THE GEMINI RISING ROCKIN' MACHINE

BOOK ONE: WHO AM I?

Book One: Who Am I?
Copyright 2016 by The Gemini Rising Rockin' Machine

ISBN-13: 978-0615900315 (Gemini Rising Rockin' Machine, The)
ISBN-10: 0615900313

For questions, comments you may send correspondence to.

thegeminirisingrockinmachine@twc.com

Official Website
www.thegeminirisingrockinmachine.com

BOOK ONE: WHO AM I? (Pages 2-46)

(Synopsis)

(SIDE ONE)
Who Am I?: Amnesia, Very sad.
Shout (Your Day Will Come): Work harder and you can make it.
A Race Called Man: Human race as a whole how we love, hate and fear.
Cursed Years: A person who is cursed to walk this earth until the end of
time, hears and sees all but can not react.
Why: Sick, doctor, pill not the results you expect.

(SIDE TWO)
All I Need: You and only you.
I Must Go Away: Leaving someone out of love or is it cowardliness?
Love Den (Not A Sin): Lovin' within Purgatory.
Angel Eyes: Finding true love within Purgatory?
Rock and Roll House: My pad in the late 80's.

(SIDE THREE)
I'll Be Your Hero: Your help is for sale.
Hero: Don't need one be one for yourself.
Me Myself & I: Living on the streets.
I'm Dying and It's Raining: Wrong place wrong time.
We the People: Do we still have a voice?

(SIDE FOUR)
Speak As One: All of us get together and be as one.
Across the Sky: Freedom VS People that want to destroy us.
I Am Wolf: Living your life as a Werewolf.
Rip You Apart While Drinking You Down: Living as a Vampire.
Bleeding My Beast Blood Upon the Floor: Evil entity living within you
**(This song is for Entertainment only. If you are contemplating suicide
please tell someone or get some help.)**

(Meaning of my Name)
Gemini - Because I am One and for its Meaning of Two
which I Use as my Muse while Writing.
Rising - To Constantly use so I never Stop trying
to Ascend to Be and do Better.
Rockin' - Is what I like to Do and What this is all About.
Machine - Is a Reminder for Myself to keep Going on
Even when Life is at its Hardest.

The numbers after the song titles are the original numbering.

(SIDE ONE)
01. Who Am I? (67.)
02. Shout (Your Day Will Come) (70.)
03. A Race Called Man (02.)
04. Cursed Years (45.)
05. Why (77.)

(SIDE TWO)
06. All I Need (41.)
07. I Must Go Away (01.)
08. Love Den (Not A Sin) (78.)
    Love Den (Not A Sin) (2.0 Version) **(693.)**
09. Angel Eyes (79.)
10. Rock And Roll House (73.)
    I Remember Rock And Roll **(906.)** (New Cover Bonus)

(SIDE THREE)
11. I'll Be Your Hero (75.)
12. Hero (74.)
13. Me Myself & I (26.)
14. I'm Dying And It's Raining (47.)
15. We The People (59.)
    So Blue **(838.)** (New Cover Bonus)

(SIDE FOUR)
16. Speak As One (54.)
17. Across The Sky (03.)
18. I Am Wolf (08.)
19. Rip You Apart While Drinking You Down (49.)
20. Bleeding My Beast Blood Upon The Floor (07.)

(Bonus Songs)
Here I Stand **(841.)** (New Cover Bonus)
Pretty Faced Bastard (Kayden's Song) **(842.)** (New Cover Bonus)
Speak As One (Original Version)

01. Who Am I?

What-Did-I-Do – Got-Myself-Into
Did-I-See the Wrong-Thing – I-Just-Don't-Know

Ticking-Away – This-Empty – Mind of Mine
It's-All-Gone – Who-I-Was
What-Did-I-Do – Do-I-Have-Anyone
That-Loves-Me – Missing-Me
Perhaps-Even – Looking-For-Me

I-Got to Get – Out of Here
They're-Not – Telling-Me-Anything
They-Have – No-Idea – Who-I-Am
What to Do – With-Me
Feel-Like a Criminal or Part-Of a Sideshow

(Chorus #1)
Who Am I – Do You Know
Do I Really Want You To Tell Me
Am I Better Off Not Knowing
Who Am I

I-See-Fear and Sadness – In-Their-Eyes
They-Keep-Talking – Trying to Put-Something
In-My-Head – So-I-Can – Go-On
Being-Able to Pay-My-Own-Way

I'm-In so Much-Pain – I-Was-Found
By-The-Side – Of a Lonely-Old-Road
Nothing-Like-This – Has-Ever-Happened
The-Whole-Life of This-Road – I'm-The-First
The-Big-Gossip of This-Town's-Population

(Chorus #2)
Who Am I
I Am The Man That Has No Past
Laughing At Nothing
And Nothing Is Funny
Who Am I
I Can't Even Remember
The Dreams That Wake Me Screaming
Please Tell Me – Who I Am

4

What-Did-I-Do – Got-Myself-Into
Did-I-See the Wrong-Thing – I-Just-Don't-Know

Think so Hard – Nothing-Comes
But-More-Questions – Why-I-Don't-Know
This-Thought is Getting-Too-Much
For-Some to Believe-Anymore

I-Might-Not-Know
Who – Why – When – What or Where
But-Their-Eyes – Are-Clear as Truth
No-Matter-What – Their-Words-Say

(Chorus #1)
Who Am I – Do You Know
Do I Really Want You To Tell Me
Am I Better Off Not Knowing
Who Am I

The-Heavy – From-This-Amnesia is Too-Much
No-Way – I'm-Gonna-Take a Chance-That
Some-Ugly – Might-Take-Away – Everything
I-Hardly-Have-Anything and I'm-Keeping-That

I'm-Out of Here – Can't-Let-Nothing or No-One
Get-In-My-Way – I've-Got to Find – My-Answers
I'm-Out of This – Medical-Hell – Have to Find-Something
My-Mind – Can-Remember-Again or For-The-First-Time
I-Just-Don't-Know – This-Scares the Hell – Out of Me

(Chorus #2)
Who Am I
I Am The Man That Has No Past
Laughing At Nothing
And Nothing Is Funny
Who Am I
I Can't Even Remember
The Dreams That Wake Me Screaming
Please Tell Me – Who I Am

What-Did-I-Do – Got-Myself-Into
Did-I-See the Wrong-Thing – I-Just-Don't-Know

Some-One-Yells – Out a Name
It's-Always the Same – It's-Not-Me
That-They – Are-Calling-For
I've-Tried to Get – Close to Someone
I-Always-End-It – Before it Goes – Too-Far

Can't-Help-Feeling-Jealous – Even if It's-Bad
It's-Still a Past – I-Could – Go-On-From-That
No-One-Understands – What-It's-Like
To-Get to Rewrite – The-Sad-Play – That-Is-My-Life
I'd-Rather-Have the Original-First-Draft
So-I-Can-Finally – Stand-Still and Absorb-It-In

(Chorus #1)
Who Am I – Do You Know
Do I Really Want You To Tell Me
Am I Better Off Not Knowing
Who Am I

It's-Been a Few-Weeks – I-Keep-Going-On
Town to Town – I-Barely-Rest
Big-Cities – Small-Towns
All-I-Know-Now – Are-Things
That-I-Like and Things-I-Don't

I'll-Keep-Going-On – Even-If-It's-Only
To-Find-Out – Am-I the Same-Person – Now
That-I-Don't – Remember-Being-Before
Will-This-Craziness – Ever-End
Don't-I – Have the Right to Find-Out

(Chorus #2)
Who Am I
I Am The Man That Has No Past
Laughing At Nothing
And Nothing Is Funny
Who Am I
I Can't Even Remember
The Dreams That Wake Me Screaming
Please Tell Me – Who I Am

What-Did-I-Do – Got-Myself-Into
Did-I-See the Wrong-Thing – I-Just-Don't-Know

Someone – Tell-Me-Already
So-I-Can – Go-On-With-My-Life
I-Have-Suffered-Enough
My-Time-Limit of Not-Knowing
Has-Surely – Been-Up-By-Now

Crazy-Has-Left-Town – Already
And-Madness is Slowly – Setting-Up-Shop
Brick by Brick – It-Goes-Up
My-Mind – Can't-Keep-Up
It-Will-Finally – Run-Out of Detours
And-Come-To a Full-Stop

(Chorus #1)
Who Am I – Do You Know
Do I Really Want You To Tell Me
Am I Better Off Not Knowing
Who Am I

Ticking-Away – This-Empty – Mind of Mine – It's-All-Gone
Who-I-Was – What-Did-I-Do – Do-I-Have-Anyone
Do-You-Know – Do-I-Want-You to Tell-Me
Or-Am-I – Better-Off-Not-Knowing

One-Last-Time – I-Ask-This-World
Who-Am-I – Who-Am-I
Not-Knowing is Slowly-Killing
The-Man – That I've-Become
I-Need an Awakening
And-For-This – Damn-Amnesia to Stop

(Chorus #2)
Who Am I
I Am The Man That Has No Past
Laughing At Nothing
And Nothing Is Funny
Who Am I
I Can't Even Remember
The Dreams That Wake Me Screaming
Please Tell Me – Who I Am

7

02. Shout (Your Day Will Come)

Here is Another-Year
All-Wrapped-Up – With-Newness
Ready-For-You to Discover
If-You-Got – What-It-Takes
To-Live-Life – To its Fullest
Work-Harder – Earn-More
Let-Your-Life – Be-Taken-Over
Your-Day – Will-Come

(Chorus)
Shout – Shout It Out – That You Matter
Shout – Shout It Out – That You Can Do It
Shout – Shout It Out – No Matter What
Stands In Your Way – Your Day Will Come

Family and Wife – Are-Complaining
They-Miss-You so Much
No-More – Time for Fun
You've-Been – Working so Hard
Finally-Having – Some-Extra
Family-Has to Understand – You're-Doing-It
All-For-Them – Your-Day-Will-Come

(Chorus)
Shout – Shout It Out – That You Matter
Shout – Shout It Out – That You Can Do It
Shout – Shout It Out – No Matter What
Stands In Your Way – Your Day Will Come

Smile-Man – Your-Day-Has-Come
You-Finally – Want for Nothing
So-What – If-You're – All-Alone
Your-Worth – Is a Mighty-Might
That-Your-Family – Couldn't-Handle
Enjoy-Your-New-Life – You've-Earned-It

(Chorus)
Shout – Shout It Out – That You Matter
Shout – Shout It Out – That You Can Do It
Shout – Shout It Out – No Matter What
Stands In Your Way – Your Day Will Come

8

03. A Race Called Man

We-Have the Power of Global-Death
One-Quick-Silver-Flash and We-Are-All-Dead
That-Thought is Inside-Us – How-Scared-We-Are
The-Boiling-Point – Has-Been – Critical-For so Long
We-All-Walk-Around – With-Happy-Hazy-Faces

We-Take-Our – Lives-Hands – To-Pick-Up – That-Child
The-Circle of Life – Goes-On and On
Some-Live for The-Day – While-Others – Wilt Away
We-May-Never-Know – The-Answer – To it All
Will-Keep-Going-On – What-Choice – Do-We-Have

(Chorus)
We Are A Race Called Man
We Love – Hate – Lust and Kill
With Compassion Of Saints
And A Killer Instinct For Bait
We Are A Race Called Man
We Are Like Shepherds With Flocks
Or Like A Beast On A Butcher's Block
We Are A Race Called Man
We Don't Know Why We're Here
Some Big Accident – We Fear

Is-Populating-The-World – The-Reason-We're-Here
Love of One-Another – We-Want
But-Death – We-Welcome as Well
We-Have-Come a Long-Way – But-Far – We-Must-Go
If-We-Ever-Want – To-Be-Like
The-Gods – Who-Supposedly – Put-Us-Here

(Chorus)
We Are A Race Called Man
We Love – Hate – Lust and Kill
With Compassion Of Saints
And A Killer Instinct For Bait
We Are A Race Called Man
We Are Like Shepherds With Flocks
Or Like A Beast On A Butcher's Block
We Are A Race Called Man
We Don't Know Why We're Here
Some Big Accident – We Fear

04. Cursed Years

I-Walk – This-Earth
Just-Like – I-Have-For so Long
Roaming is All – I-Am-Damned to Do
To-See-All – That-I-Have-Seen
Is a Fantasy – It's a Nightmare

To-Know – All-I-Know
Never-Able to React
Is a Hell – That-Never-Ends
I-Made a Mistake – I-Cannot-Correct
Now-I'm-Cursed – Now-I'm-Damned

(Chorus)
Nothing Is All I Have
All These Cursed Years
I Can't Take Any More
And It Never Stops
Please God End My Afterlife
Or End My Cursed Years
By Letting Me Enter Heaven

So-Many – Never-Notice-Me
I-Am-There – Not at All
So-Lonely – For-Much-Too-Long
Think-I'm-Insane – Can a Soul – Be-Insane

Oh to Be-Able to Touch
Just-One of The-Many – Beautiful-Ladies
That-Have-Blessed – My-Eyes
With-Their-Wonderfulness
It-Would-Be-Nice – Even-Only
To-Have a Drink – And a Laugh

(Chorus)
Nothing Is All I Have
All These Cursed Years
I Can't Take Any More
And It Never Stops
Please God End My Afterlife
Or End My Cursed Years
By Letting Me Enter Heaven

Lord – God
I-Made a Mistake – I-Cannot-Correct
You-Cursed-Me – You-Damned-Me

Watching – The-Ultimate-Sin
Did-Nothing – Only-That
Your-Son – Our-Savior – Killed by Hate
Killed by Fear by Those-He-Loved

I-Am-Sorry – Please-Forgive-Me
I-Feared for My-Life – Now-Know
It-Should-Have-Been – For-My-Soul
Let-Me-Go-Back – Right-My-Wrong
Let-Me-Die – Please-End-My-Curse

(Chorus)
Nothing Is All I Have
All These Cursed Years
I Can't Take Any More
And It Never Stops
Please God End My Afterlife
Or End My Cursed Years
By Letting Me Enter Heaven

Lord – God
Angry-Men – With-Spikes – Pounded
Their-Spikes – Into-Flesh – Using-Rocks
Angry-Men – Carried-Spears
That-Kept the Crowd in Line

Spears-That-Stabbed – Many-Watchers
Including – Through the Body of Christ
I-Watched – I-Cried – I-Was-Frozen – With-Fear
If-I'd-Helped – I-Would-Have-Been-Killed

(Chorus)
Nothing Is All I Have
All These Cursed Years
I Can't Take Any More
And It Never Stops
Please God End My Afterlife
Or End My Cursed Years
By Letting Me Enter Heaven

05. Why

I-Feel-Sick and Weak – In this Doctor's-Office
Gathering-My-Strength – For-When-My-Name is Called
I'm-Looked-Over – Many-Questions-Later
I'm-Sent-Away to Give-Up – My-Blood for Testing
Laid-Around in Pain – Waiting for The-Answer
The-Call-Came – Painfully-I-Returned
Told-Some-Horrible-News – But-Not to Worry
It-Won't-Make-Me – Die-Too-Soon – and
They-Have-Something – They-Want to Try-On-Me

Pills-For-Pain – Pills-For-Nausea – and
The-Pill-That-Cures and Gives-Even-More
A-Freaking-Look – At-The-Other-Side
I-Did-Not – Ask for This – Just-Wanted to Feel-Better
Doctor-Gave-Me a Pill – Made-My-Life a Living-Hell
Now-I-See-Angels – Sounds-Great-Don't-It – But-No
It-Sucks – They-Are-Not-Very-Nice – They-Do-Not
Want to Be-Seen – Makes-Them-Mad and Hostile

(Chorus)
Why – I Don't Understand
Why God – Why
Can You Not Undo This
Let Me Live My Life In Peace

If-I-See an Angel – I-Go-Up to Them
They-Either-Take-Off or Try to Attack-Me
Always a Look of Disbelief – In-Their-Eyes
They-Have-No-Idea – Why-I'm-Like-This

My-Blood-Disorder – Is the Reason-Why – I-Know
That-All-This – Has-Happened to Me – I'm-Left
Alone-Now – No-More-Tapping of Me – Don't-Know-If
That is Good or Bad – Every-Time – I-Ask an Angel
They-Now-Go-On – Like-I'm-Not – Even-There
Is-This an Order or Am-I a Punch-Line for God

(Chorus)
Why – I Don't Understand
Why God – Why
Can You Not Undo This
Let Me Live My Life In Peace
12

06. All I Need

This-Lonely-Night – Begs-For-Love
The-Love-That-We – Share-Together
Is-Like-No-Other – On-This-Earth
Baby-It's-Time – Our-Pause-Stopped

These-Long-Nights – Without-You
It's-All-I-Can-Do – Not to Lose-Control
I-Miss-You – You're-All-I – Think-About
We're-Going-To – Be-Together
Make-Loving – Like-Nothing-Happened

(Chorus)
'Cause Baby You're All I Need
To Make Me Feel So Right
I Can Go Through Anything
There's Nothing That I Won't Do
'Cause Baby You're All I Need

Let's-Forget – Our-Mistakes
We're-Better – With-The-Other
Your-Eyes – Your-Voice – Tells-Me
You've-Missed-Me – Baby
Let's-Get-Back – To-The-Good-Life

Many-Have – Just-Loneliness
They'll-Never-Know – What-We-Have
For-Peace and Harmony – Baby
Let's-Not – Just-Make-Love
To-Each-Other – Let's-Make-Love
For-The-Whole – Wide-World-To-Feel

(Chorus)
'Cause Baby You're All I Need
To Make Me Feel So Right
I Can Go Through Anything
There's Nothing That I Won't Do
'Cause Baby You're All I Need

07. I Must Go Away

Every-Time – I-Look at Your-Face
Your-Lovely-Embrace – It-Grounds-Me
If-I-Ever-Want to Be-My-Own
Something of Substance

Something – That is Proud to Be
I-Know-What – I-Must-Do
Set-You-Free – Alone-I-Shall-Be

(Chorus)
I Must Go Away – I'm Tearing You Apart
I Must Go Away – It's In Your Eyes
I Must Go Away – I Can See What I've Done
I Must Go Away – Before I Break You

No-One-Understands – The-Pain-I'm-In
Guilty of Everything – Guilty of Nothing
I-Know – I-Was-Never-Perfect
Had a Path – I-Did-Not-Take

Never-Allowed – My-Own-Mistakes
Sheltered – Held-Back – From-This-World
I-Was-Lost – You-Found-Me
I-Know-What – I-Must-Do
Set-You-Free – Alone-I-Shall-Be

(Chorus)
I Must Go Away – I'm Tearing You Apart
I Must Go Away – It's In Your Eyes
I Must Go Away – I Can See What I've Done
I Must Go Away – Before I Break You

You're-Such a Beautiful-Person
I-Know-You – You-Will-Take-It
I-Will-Remember – All-The-Years
Undying-Love – You-Gave to Me
Undying Love – Unselfishly

Remember-I-Will – Always-Love-You
I-Know-What – I-Must-Do
Set-You-Free – Alone-I-Shall-Be

14

(Chorus)
I Must Go Away – I'm Tearing You Apart
I Must Go Away – It's In Your Eyes
I Must Go Away – I Can See What I've Done
I Must Go Away – Before I Break You

Please – Pretty-Baby
Don't-Cry – I'm-Not-Worth-It
I'm a Disaster – I'm-Broken
You-Should-Have so Much-More
For-All – You've-Given to Me

Make a Life of Your-Own
You-Deserve-It – You-Need-It
If-I-Stay – I'll-Darken-Your-Aura
Erase – That-Was-You – Before-Me
I-Know-What – I-Must-Do
Set-You-Free – Alone-I-Shall-Be

(Chorus)
I Must Go Away – I'm Tearing You Apart
I Must Go Away – It's In Your Eyes
I Must Go Away – I Can See What I've Done
I Must Go Away – Before I Break You

Every-Time – I-Look at Your-Face
Your-Lovely-Embrace – It-Grounds-Me
If-I-Ever-Want to Be-My-Own
Something of Substance

Something – That is Proud to Be
I-Know-What – I-Must-Do
Set-You-Free – Alone-I-Shall-Be

(Chorus)
I Must Go Away – I'm Tearing You Apart
I Must Go Away – It's In Your Eyes
I Must Go Away – I Can See What I've Done
I Must Go Away – Before I Break You

(From Purgatory's Full: A Song, A Dream Or A Cold Hard Reality, In Thirty-Six Parts.)

I feel so beastly turned on from this sweet scent in the air around me. Starting to salivate, wow, I have never been this turned on before. I'm starting to pant, a deep instinctual roar comes roaring out of me. Swimming to the shore as fast as I can, I shake myself off and grab up my spiked bat, leaving my clothes behind. Naked, I take off running. Damn am I running fast, leaving imprints on the ground, I'm so turned on. I have to meet all the women that are sending out their intoxicating scents.

(Kayden, free from the touch of evil but remembering what the Hell Witch did for him by helping him remember sex. What a nasty let down it was when he did but he is still glad he has remembered. Kayden, is all in for War, never letting himself have but a few minutes and by doing this he has missed out on a lot, he now has discovered. Kayden just like a lot of other men is running to the Love Den, a place created by a very smart lady named Rebecka, where ladies let men come in and have a good time. They can stay as long as they want and all it costs them is some of their power. Strong ones lose a lot of power but they survive, the weak ones, well the surrounding woods has a spot filled up with their clothes, while all the ladies enjoy their power ups. As for Kayden, well let's find out, shall we?)

The wonderful scent stops at this lonely cabin in the woods. My mind takes back over my sex drive. I walk around the cabin, got to be smart can not let myself be so easily fooled, everything seems nice and quiet. Getting back to the front door, no one was in waiting still something isn't quite right, so I walk into the woods surrounding the cabin, no scents of death, but there is something else that I smell and about a mile away I spot what I smelled, mounds and mounds of clothes everywhere, now I get it, they're another kind of Witch, a more softer and hopefully more desirable kind. Well I'm no prude, everybody has to earn a living and everyone wants to win this War in Purgatory.

I don't know what's going on but I'm going to find out. The good thing about this is, I'm not feeling freaked out. The Hell Witch has dulled me. I can tell I've changed and I'm even more willing to do whatever it takes to win this War in Purgatory, but for now I will also have some fun.

I walk over to one of the mounds of clothes and see if anything fits. After I get dressed I walk back to the cabin filled with waiting women.

I'm at the door, I open it without knocking, like I own the place. Closing the door behind me, I hear, "Welcome to the Love Den, I'm your host Rebecka. Have you been here before or is this your first time?" Rebecka is gorgeous. This is so different, for so long all I did was kill now all I want to do is something else and very much at that. I tell Rebecka this is my first time and she is mine for the night. She steps back putting her hands up saying, "Slow down there honey we have to take care of business first. There are rules, no killing and taking powers from any of the ladies that work here at the Love Den. These special ladies are for sexual pleasure only, no hurting them or falling in love with them or trying to take them away from the Love Den. You are welcome to stay as long as you want but the cost for this is some of your power. The longer you stay the more power you have to pay and the Love Den is not responsible if you stay too long and it costs you all the power that you have, you still owe it to us. You have to agree to this but at least you'll be happy before you burn."

I stop walking and look at sexy Rebecka, she laughs and says, "You didn't think this was for free did you? I guess you thought because of who you are and since you are so turned on that you can come in here and take what you want? Well stranger, it does not work that way. No way, ever." I tell her, "My name is Kayden." Rebecka asks, "Kayden Hart?" I say, "Oh yeah." and tell her what she can do with her rules and I will not be giving up any of my powers. I will play all I want and won't pay a cent of power. Then I tell Rebecka while grabbing this little hottie walking by that I will start my time here at the Love Den with both of them first.

08. Love Den (Not A Sin)

I-Came to The-Love-Den
For-Some-Fun – Staying
Enjoying-Them-All – For-Hours
And-Hours – Finish-With-One
Enjoy-The-Next – Love-Den-Lady

I'm a Big-Powered-Up – Dead-Man
So-Turned-On – It's-Been so Long
Can't'-Believe – I-Forgot-Sex
Very-Glad – That-It's-Back – Within-My-Mind

Had to Take a Dip – In a Lake
Just a Moment to Relax
And-It-All – Came-Back to Me
I've-Been-Killing – For so Long
Just so I-Can-Be – The-Last-One
Now-I-Have a Release – Within-Purgatory

(Chorus)
At The Love Den – Sex Is On The Menu
Take All You Want – All It Cost Is Power
Stay Too Long – The Love Den Ladies
Will Suck You Dry – Of All Your Power

Purgatory-Became a Hell-For-Us
There-Can-Be – Only-One-Left
All-Others – Are-Killed and Sent to Hell
Thinking of Nothing-Else
Until-I-Met-Up – With-The-Hell-Witch

She-Almost – Destroyed-My-Mind
Don't-Know-What – I-Would-Have-Done
If-Not-For – The-Scent of The-Love-Den-Ladies
It-Led-Me-Straight-Here to The-Love-Den
So-I-Could-Take – What-I-Needed – So-Bad

(Chorus)
At The Love Den – Sex Is On The Menu
Take All You Want – All It Cost Is Power
Stay Too Long – The Love Den Ladies
Will Suck You Dry – Of All Your Power

18

Love Den (Not A Sin) (2.0 Version) (693.)

Sirens – Are-Calling-Me
With-Their – Sexy-Scent
Leading-Me to The-Love-Den
Which is Not a Sin

Succubus – Are-These-Ladies
That-Tempt-You – With-Their-Bodies
They-Let-You – Have-Their-Love
All-It-Cost-You – Is-Some of Your-Power
Stay-Too-Long – You-Will-Die

(Chorus)
The Love Den Is Not A Sin
If You Are Turned On
Come To The Love Den
Stay As Long As You Can
If You Have Enough – Power In You
To Handle – The Love Den Ladies

At-The-Love-Den – You-Can
Have-One – You-Can-Have – Them-All
They-Will-Excite-You – They-Will-Punish-You
They-Will-Make-You-Feel – Like-You're – In-Control

While-Your-Lusting – Try to Remember
While-You're – Getting-Weaker
They're-Getting-Stronger – By-The-Moment
As-Soon as You Drop – Your-Lusting
Is-Over-With – You're-Dead
As-Your-Horny-Soul – Falls to Hell

(Chorus)
The Love Den Is Not A Sin
If You Are Turned On
Come To The Love Den
Stay As Long As You Can
If You Have Enough – Power In You
To Handle – The Love Den Ladies

(Repeat Chorus)

19

(From Purgatory's Full: A Song, A Dream Or A Cold Hard Reality, In Thirty-Six Parts.)

Angel Eyes appears with bags in hand, when she reaches me she drops them on the floor and jumps into my arms, kissing me madly, I kiss her the same way right in front of Rebecka and all the other ladies of the Love Den. Concerned and raging voices, shout out don't do this Angel Eyes, he'll use you and then he will kill you when he gets tired of you. Don't be a fool Angel Eyes, you don't love him, you just think you do. Stay here where you are safe at the Love Den with all of us. We love you, need you and we will protect you.

Angel Eyes stops kissing me, looks me in my eyes and smiles so nice and sexy. Then she says to all, still looking me straight in my eyes, "I don't care. I love him, I love his power and I love his manhood. Kayden Hart is the man in Purgatory made for me and only for me. If he ever wants my life, to go along with my heart that he already owns so be it. I will gladly give it to him because I believe so deeply inside myself that Kayden is very special and chosen by God to win this War. That he is so great and God likes him so much that he will give Kayden a special favor if he asks God for it. If my love is true enough and Kayden still wants it, he'll ask God if I can come to Heaven with him instead of killing me and sending me to Hell."

Angel Eyes climbs off me, looks back into my eyes, telling me that she will take care of me. And that after a long day of hunting and killing, she will have a great meal waiting for me and when I walk in the door she will have a beer waiting in hand, wanting and willing to make love to me before we eat the meals she will always make for me. Then Angel Eyes drops to her knees and says, "Please Kayden, I'm begging you, make me yours forever and you, Kayden Hart will never want for anything ever again."

With a loving hand I pull Angel Eyes up to her feet and tell her, that I agree, that she is my sweet, sweet Angel Eyes, that I love her and I will not hurt or kill her, as long as she is true to me and never betrays me or my love. I tell Angel Eyes to only bring two bags, because we have far to travel, she grabs them and we walk out the door together, to more don't do this and please come back, we need you to stay. I close the door saying, I'll be back when I feel like splurging again.

They curse me with lots of harsh words, I smile saying finally, "Be nice ladies or I won't be when I come back."

Angel Eyes and I having been walking and talking for a few miles now as I turn to her and start singing out loud lyrics that come to my mind about her.

Oh-My-Sweet – Angel-Eyes
I-Love-You so Much
We're-going to Have-Such
Sweet-Love-Together
Oh-My-Sweet – Angel-Eyes
You're-All – That-I-Want
I-Am so Lucky to Have-You
I'll-Love-You – Forever
My-Sweet – Sweet-Angel-Eyes

So very happy, Angel Eyes screams out to me, "Again, sing it again. Please sing it again." Throwing her bags down as I start re-singing she starts to dance around looking so beautiful and singing along with me already knowing the lyrics, we are both in love and we both know the other is in love with us by the way we look each other in the eyes.

Angel Eyes stops dancing and runs over to me with such a big smile on her face and tears in her eyes, jumping into my arms kissing me like a very sexy woman that loves who she has to kiss, she stops, licks her lips and tells me that she loves me so very much. I wipe away the tears that she is trying to hide, telling her I love her too, we start kissing again and our passion rises as we start to make love outside all alone, totally free and in love, like this will be our last time that we will ever be able to make love to each other again. This is our best love making yet, as we are both giving the other the best that we have to give, I feel so great and sad as we are finishing, because I sense an army of gloom coming for me from up ahead.

09. Angel Eyes

We-Met at The-Love-Den
You-Were-Special – Compared to The-Rest
Those-Blue – Angel-Eyes
Your-Cute – Everything-Else
Made-Me-Fall – In-Love-With-You – So-I

Pushed-You-Away – When-We-Were-Done
Did-Not-Dare – Come-Back to You
For-I-Know – What-Purpose – You-Pose
To-Bring-Men to Their-Knees
Still-It's-Hard – Not to Look at You
While-Finishing – With-Another-Lady

(Chorus)
Angel Eyes – I Love You
Deep Down – In My Dark Heart
That Bleeds Out – Spoiled Blood
Because Of This Damn War
Angel Eyes – I Know That I Can't
Trust You – But Enjoy You – I Will
Until The Time Of Your Death

I'm-Leaving – You-Call-For-Me to Wait
All-The-Other-Ladies – Are so Mad
They-Received-None of My-Power
For-The-First-Time – Nothing but Sex
Not-Without-Trying – Did-Them-No-Good
For-I'm a Big-Powered-Up – Dead-Man
Too-Much-Even – For-All of Them to Match

Waiting-You-Run to Me – With-Bags in Hands
Jumping in My-Arms – Kissing-Me-Madly
Pulling-You in Tight – I-Lovingly-Kiss-You
They're-Yelling to Stop – Not to Do-This
Saying – I-Will-Kill-You – When-I-Get-Bored
Crying-Out – After-Pulling – Your-Lips-From-Mine
I-Don't-Care – He's-The-One – I-Love-Him
He-Can-Have – My-Life – If-He-Wants-It
I-Only-Want to Serve-Him and Feel-His-Power

22

(Chorus)
Angel Eyes – I Love You
Deep Down – In My Dark Heart
That Bleeds Out – Spoiled Blood
Because Of This Damn War
Angel Eyes – I Know That I Can't
Trust You – But Enjoy You – I Will
Until The Time Of Your Death

Walking and Talking
Holding – Each-Others-Hands
Laughing-Away so Much-In-Love
I-Start-Singing to You – Throwing-Your
Bags-Away – You-Start-Dancing
So-Beautiful – You-Keep – My-Eyes on You

I-Stop-Singing – Walk-Up to You
Pick-Your – Sexy-Little-Figure
Up to Me and Kiss-You-Deeply
Then- I-Pick-You – Up-Higher
So-Your-Heart is Beating in My-Face
So-You-Can -Accept – Your-Fate
An-Arrow – Stuck-In-Your-Back

Sweet-Angel-Eyes – You-Were – The-Set-Up
These-Twenty or More – Are-The-Trap
Throwing-You-Down – You-Ask-Me-How
How-Could-I-Not – I-Tell-You
Walking-Away – I-Stalk-My-Prey
Let-The-Hunt – Begin – Taking-Arrow
After-Arrow – Stuck-In-My-Face and Body
I-Keep-Pulling – Them-Out – While-Marching-On
'Til-I-Have – Every-One of Their-Power-Up's

(Chorus)
Angel Eyes – I Love You
Deep Down – In My Dark Heart
That Bleeds Out – Spoiled Blood
Because Of This Damn War
Angel Eyes – I Know That I Can't
Trust You – But Enjoy You – I Will
Until The Time Of Your Death

10. Rock And Roll House

Work-Week is Over
Damn it Was a Long-One
Let-The-Weekend – Begin
Start-This – Friday-Night – Up-Right
Time-For-Beer – Women and Song

(Chorus)
Rock – Rock
Rock And Roll House
Rock – Rock
It's A Rock And Roll House
Rock – Rock
Rock And Roll House
Rock – Rock
It's A Rock And Roll House

Partying-Hearty – Real-Hard
Just – Rocking – Away
Having a Great-Time
Jamming – Holding-My-Beer
I-Have a Rocking – Good-Buzz – Going-On

(Repeat Chorus)

She-Sits – On-My-Lap
Gets-Me – Real-Hard – Real-Quick
She-Likes – What-She-Feels
It's-Time to Find a Bedroom
Looking-Forward to Pounding – My-Buzz-Away

(Chorus)
Rock – Rock
Rock And Roll House
Rock – Rock
It's A Rock And Roll House
Rock – Rock
Rock And Roll House
Rock – Rock
It's A Rock And Roll House

I Remember Rock And Roll (906.)

Memories of Long-Ago in My-Mind
Calling-Me-Back – Through-Time
To-Forget-All-My-Heavies
To-Party-Hardy and Rock-On
Like-My-Life is On-The-Line

I-Remember – Oh-Yes-I-Do
Summer-Time – Back-Seat-Loving
I-Remember – Oh-Yes-I-Do
Summer-Time – Skinny-Dipping
I-Remember – Oh-Yes-I-Do
Summer-Time – Falling in Lust
And-I-Remember – And-I-Remember
Rock – And – Roll

(Chorus)
I Remember Rock And Roll
And What It Did For My Soul
I Remember Rock And Roll
It Kept Me Young And Free
I Remember Rock And Roll
Like A Yesterday's Dream Come True
I Remember Rock And Roll
So I'm Going To Start
Rock And Rolling Again
'Til The Day I Die

Memories of Long-Ago in My-Mind
Calling-Me-Back-Through-Time
To-Forget-All-My-Heavies
To-Party-Hardy and Rock-On
Like-My-Life is On-The-Line

I-Remember – Oh-Yes-I-Do
Summer-Time – Back-Seat-Loving
I-Remember – Oh-Yes-I-Do
Summer-Time – Skinny-Dipping
I-Remember – Oh-Yes-I-Do
Summer-Time – Falling in Lust
And-I-Remember – And-I-Remember
Rock – And – Roll
(Repeat Chorus)
25

11. I'll Be Your Hero

Call-Me – If-You-Need – Some-Help
I'm a Hero – Powerful and True
I'm-Here for Whatever-You-Need
No-Matter – What-The-Danger
I'm-Here-For-You
I-Can-Do-Anything – Believe-Me

(Chorus)
I'll Be Your Hero – Yes I'm The One
I'll Be Your Hero – Yes I'm The One
As Soon As Your Payment Clears
I'll Be Your Hero

Call-Me – If-You-Need – Some-Help
I'm a Hero – Powerful and True
I'm-Just a Phone-Call-Away
Crime – Does-Not-Pay
But-You – Will-Have-To
If-You – Want-Me to Save-You

(Chorus)
I'll Be Your Hero – Yes I'm The One
I'll Be Your Hero – Yes I'm The One
As Soon As Your Payment Clears
I'll Be Your Hero

Call-Me – If-You-Need – Some-Help
I'm a Hero – Powerful and True
I'm-Out – Saving-Someone
When-You – Get-No-Answer
Leave a Message
No-Help or Price – Is-Too-Much
On-Your – Safe-Side – Better
Consider-Me – Your-Rainy-Day

(Chorus)
I'll Be Your Hero – Yes I'm The One
I'll Be Your Hero – Yes I'm The One
As Soon As Your Payment Clears
I'll Be Your Hero

12. Hero

Car-Crash – House-Fire – Bomb-Goes-Off
Somebody – Always-Needs-Saving
So-Into-Your-Life – You do Not – Pay-Attention
To-What's-Going-On – Right in Front of you
Blindly-Enter – Without-Looking

Life's-Not-Simple – It's-Really-Damn-Hard
There's so Much – Ugly-Around-Us
The-Government-Doesn't-Care to Do-Anything-About-It
Crime-Pays – Keeps-All-These – Bastards in Jobs
No-Way-Will-They – Let-This be Taken-From-Them
The-More-Killings the More-Funding-They-Get
Look-Into-Their-Eyes – You'll-See-Dollar-Signs

(Chorus)
Don't-Look At Me – I'm-Not A Hero
Save-Yourselves – I'm-Not-Your-Hero
Don't-Look At Me – I'm-Not A Hero
Save-Yourselves – I'm-Not-Your-Hero
Call-555-Hero – If-You-Need-Saving

Stabbing – Car-Jacking – Drive by Shooting
Something-Always – Going-On
Are-You-Stupid – Have-No – Common-Sense
Always-Thinking – Someone's-Going to Save-You
No-Matter – How-Deep – You-Step-In-It
You-Feel – You-Have the Right to Get-Out of It

Give-You-This – Watch-Your-Back
Never-Trust – Anyone-Fully
Have-Something – Worth-Taking
Expect-Someone – Else-Wants-It
Know-Where – Your-Children-Are
Don't-Let-Them – Drink-The-Wine – Unless-You
Want-Them – To-Become – Government's-Slaves

(Chorus)
Don't-Look At Me – I'm-Not A Hero
Save-Yourselves – I'm-Not-Your-Hero
Don't-Look At Me – I'm-Not A Hero
Save-Yourselves – I'm-Not-Your-Hero
Call-555-Hero – If-You-Need-Saving

27

13. Me Myself & I

I-Live – On-The-Streets – All-Alone
Use to Have a Family – Use to Have a Job
Now-I-Have-Nothing – But – Me-Myself & I

Sunrise-On-My-Face – Waking-Up – In a Box
The-Day's-Pain is Already-Tormenting-Me
I'm-Still a Man – No-Matter – What-You-Think

As-You-See-Me – On-Your-Way – To-Your-Day
Living-My-Life – In-The-Streets
Eating-Trash and Drinking-Drain-Water

(Chorus)
Me Myself & I Are So Lonely
Me Myself & I Are So Afraid
Me Myself & I Are So Hungry
Me Myself & I Are So Angry
Why Won't Anybody Help
Me Myself & I

I-Live – On-The-Streets – All-Alone
Use to Have a Family – Use to Have a Job
Now-I-Have-Nothing – But – Me-Myself & I

The-Bottle is My-Best-Friend
The-Bottle – Helps-Me – With-My-Fears
I-Talk to Myself – Because-I-Have – No-One

People-Point – People-Stare – They-Listen-In
On-My-Conversation – Of-One
They-Tell-Me to Shut-Up and Go-Away
They-Stomp – Their-Feet –Like-I'm a Dog

(Chorus)
Me Myself & I Are So Lonely
Me Myself & I Are So Afraid
Me Myself & I Are So Hungry
Me Myself & I Are So Angry
Why Won't Anybody Help
Me Myself & I

14. I'm Dying And It's Raining

This-Day – Sucked-Bad
The-Boss – Was an Ass – All-Day
When-I-Finally – Get-Home
No-Wife – No-Dinner
Just a Another – Day of Paradise
That-Makes-Me – Want to Scream

Pity-Party is About to Start
Forget-That – Bar or Six-Pack
I-Want-Some-Suds to Wash-This
Piece of Crap – Day-All-Away

(Chorus)
I'm Dying And It's Raining
What The Hell Did I Do
But Come Here To Pick Up Some Beer
They Didn't Even Take My Money
I Am Shot For Being In The Way
It's Not Fair – I'm Dying And It's Raining

Get-Out of My-Car – Walk-Up to The-Door
Pushed-Away – From it With-Force
I-Feel a Sharp-Sting – In-My-Chest
Such a Loud-Sound – Drifting-Away
To-Running-Feet – On-The-Wet-Pavement

People-Are-Walking – Up-To-Me
They're so Close – I-Can't-Breathe
I-Look-Over – With-Pain – Watching-My
Blood-Flowing – Away-From-Me
Mixing-With – The-Rain
And-Starting a Bloody-Stream
I-Wish – I-Would-Have – Went-To a Bar

(Chorus)
I'm Dying And It's Raining
What The Hell Did I Do
But Come Here To Pick Up Some Beer
They Didn't Even Take My Money
I Am Shot For Being In The Way
It's Not Fair – I'm Dying And It's Raining

29

15. We The People

We-Walk-Alone – In-This-Life
Trying to Find – Our-Easy-End
It's-Been – Very-Long
Since-We-Felt – Any-Peace
Will-This-Ever-Stop – Everything – Taken-Away
While-We-Feel – Betrayed and Alone

I'm-Just-One of The-Many
That-The-World – Has-Tried to Erase
Forgotten-About – Nothing-More
My-Life – Has-No-Worth – I'm-Gonna-Change-That
I-Believe – I'm-Something – Brand-New

(Chorus)
We The People
There Needs To Be More
For People – That Have Nothing
We The People
We Are Very Poor
Why Don't You – Understand This
We The People
Are Tired Of Having Nothing
While Others Have It All

The-Rich – Gets-Richer
While-The-Poor – Stays-Poor
Is-This-Fair – Is-This – The-American-Way
Yesterday – Maybe-Today – But-Not
Tomorrow – No-Tomorrow – Things-Will
Have to Change or This-Country – Will-Fall
It-Will-Die – From-All-Its – Hateful-Greed

(Chorus)
We The People
There Needs To Be More
For People – That Have Nothing
We The People
We Are Very Poor
Why Don't You – Understand This
We The People
Are Tired Of Having Nothing
While Others Have It All

So Blue (838.)

Sunshine – On-My-Face
Makes-No-Difference
I'm-Out of Place – Don't-Want
To be Around-Here – Anymore

Mankind-Has-Changed
Earth is At a Boiling-Point
Hate – Hate – Hate
Is-The-New – Peace and Freedom

(Chorus)
I'm So Blue
Ain't That So True
What The Hell Can I Do
No Space-Ship In Sight
Damn This Crap-Hole Of A World
I'm So Blue – Screw You
I'm So Blue – Screw You All
Screw The World – I'm So Blue

I-Was-Out and About
Just-Doing – My-Thing
People-Came – Up to Me
Told-Me – I-Don't-Belong-There
With a Face – Like-Mine

Now-I'm a Pissed – Off-Spirit
That-Wants – His-Revenge
Hope-You're-Feeling
More-Than – Just-Blue

(Chorus #2)
I'm So Blue
Ain't That So True
I'm Freaking Dead
All Because Of A Mob Of Haters
That Killed Me On Their Way
To Hate Some More And More
I'm So Blue – Screw You
I'm So Blue – Screw You All
Screw The World – I'm So Blue

31

16. Speak As One

Come-On-Everybody
Stop-Being so Down
Time to Raise-Up – Some-Fire
The-Fire – That-Burns – Inside-Us-All
Know-Damn-Well – That-You-Feel-It
What-You – Gonna-Do-About- It
Just-Sit – Eat – Crap – Then-Repeat

No-Way-Man – I'm-Not-Down – With-That
I-Gotta-Be-Me – The-One and Only
Look at Me – With- Hate – It-Goes-Straight-Through
And-Leaves – No-Scars – Yeah-Right – Fuck-It

(Chorus)
Speak – Speak As One
They Have Nothing For That
Total Power Are We
When We Speak As One
Come Together Everybody
Let's Speak As One – Like-We're-One

Don't-Matter – What-This-Time
The-System – Has to Bring – Us-Down
Don't-Matter – Who-We-Are
If-We're-Working or Poor
With-Shelter or Not – We're-All-Prey

Right-Wants-Us – To-Pray
Kneel-To-God's-Way
Pray-For-Everything
Left-Wants-Us – To-Bow
To-All-Their – Great-Power
Thankful-For-Everything

You-Know-What – I-Say-To-Both
No-Way-Man – Don't-Want-Either
Does-Not-Fit – My-Life-Style
Time-For-Both – To-Scoot
Out-Of-The-Way
For-Our-New-Day – And-Way

32

(Chorus)
Speak – Speak As One
They Have Nothing For That
Total Power Are We
When We Speak As One
Come Together Everybody
Let's Speak As One – Like-We're-One

Anarchy-You-Scream – At-We
We're-Not-Listening – This-Time
We're-Not-Afraid – See-We-Not-Shake
Revolution – Giants-Will-Fall
When-We – Speak-As-One
You-With-The – Power-Of-God
You-With-The – All-Power
Cannot-Touch-Us – Anymore
Our-Eyes – Are-20/20
We-Can-Hear – The-Needle – When-Dropped

Bring-Your-Bibles – Bring-Your-War-Machines
We'll-Bring – Only-Ourselves – Our-Votes
We-Will-Make – Our-Stand
No-More of This-Crap
Make-You – Taste-Reality

You-Are – The-Nothing
We-Are-The-Power – See-You-Shake
You-Can't-Believe – This-Is-Happening
We-Can – We-Have-No-Doubt
We-Speak – As-One
Millions-Of-Us – As-One
What-Did-You-Think – Would-Happen

(Chorus)
Speak – Speak As One
They Have Nothing For That
Total Power Are We
When We Speak As One
Come Together Everybody
Let's Speak As One – Like-We're-One

17. Across The Sky

One-Quick-Silver-Flash – Devastation is Here
Bomb of Death – Has-Pummeled – The-Ground
Turning-Flesh and Rock to Dust
No-More-Picnics – In-The-Sun

Dumb-People of Authority
Have-Let-Us-Down – For-The-Last-Time
Now-It's-Too-Late – Mother-Earth
Screaming and Burning – On-Fire
Ready to Spread – Nuclear-Winter

(Chorus)
Across The Sky
Holy Crap What Is It
Death Is The Answer
Across The Sky
What Have We Done
Our Shadows Burn To The Ground

We-Think – For-Thou-We-Are
Not-Enough – Not-Yesterday
No-Graves – For-The-Dead – Just-Death
Everywhere – For-No-One to Notice
Live and Let-Live – Not to Get-Involved
Has-Made-Us-Dead– It's-Too-Late – It's-Over
Such-Precious-Foresight – Could-Have-Saved-Us

Death-Merchants – Killing-Sprees
Dying-World – Bleeds-Every-Day
Killing-Death – Is-Not-Fun – For-Anyone
If-There is Survival – Will-They – Make a Vow
To-Stop-Evil – In-All-Its-Evil – Hateful-Forms
So-Freedom – Can-Reign-Free – Another-Day

(Chorus)
Across The Sky
Holy Crap What Is It
Death Is The Answer
Across The Sky
What Have We Done
Our Shadows Burn To The Ground

34

18. I Am Wolf

Knocked-Down to The-Ground
It-Pounced – Unseen
Tears at Me – Bites-Down-Hard
My-Flesh – Already-Torn

Awaken-From-Shock – Fighting-Back
I-Will-Not – Die-This-Way – No-Wolf
Out of The-Night – Will-Devour-Me
I-Bite its Nose – Poke its Eyes
Just-Enough to Break-Free

It's a Big-Bad-Beast – Standing-Erect
Looking-Down at Me – With-I-Swear
A-Grin – On its Brow – Its-Tongue
Hanging-Out – Dripping-Blood
The-Wolf's-Stance – I-Know – Will-Not be Long
But-Its-Eyes – Eternity – Dwells in Them

It-Snaps-Forward – With a Low-Growl
For-Battle and Blood-Lust is What it Wants
I-Know – Death-Has-Come to Me – With-Teeth
Then a Shot – Out of The-Night – It's-Dead

(Chorus)
I Am Wolf – I Can Smell Prey In The Air
My First Time – In What Will Come To Be
Many Lunar – Cycles I'll Dance To
Many Of Deaths – I Will Be – The Cause Of
For I Am Wolf – Just Let Me – Live Free

Old-Man – Staring at Me
Double-Barrel – Empty-Smoking
Silver-Pellets – He-Says to Me
Look in His-Eyes – I'm-Still – Going to Die
Sorry-Young-One – The-Bite is In-You
You-Have to Die – Better-Now – Than-Later
The-Beast – You-Will-Become
I-Cannot – Will-Not – Let-You-Kill

Only-One-Chance – It's-My-Turn to Pounce
I-Did-Not – Ask for This – I-Want to Live
The-Old-Man's-Throat – Is-In-My-Hands

35

I-Lay-Him-Down – Beside the Beast
Now-There-Are – Two-Men-Dead – On-The-Ground
No-Beast-Insight – But-Apparently-Me
I-Am-Wolf– I-Am-Wolf-Now – Just-Let-Me-Be
I-Run – With-The-Wind to My-Home
I'm-Fevered – Up-With-Fear
My-Mind is Racing – Faster-Than – My-Body

(Chorus)
I Am Wolf – I Can Smell Prey In The Air
My First Time – In What Will Come To Be
Many Lunar – Cycles I'll Dance To
Many Of Deaths – I Will Be – The Cause Of
For I Am Wolf – Just Let Me – Live Free

Awake – I-Feel so Good so Refreshed
(Must-Have-Been a Dream)
How-Long – Have-I-Slept – It's-Night
The-Next-Night – I-Come to Find-Out
(Must-Have-Been a Dream)
Almost a Month-Now – No-Worries in Sight
(Just a Dream – Did-I-Even – Dream-It at All)

Full-Moon – In-The-Sky – So-Bright and Clear
There's an Itch – Inside-Me – Now it Starts to Burn
I-Begin to Creak and Crack – Hairs-Begin to Grow
With-Each-New-Strand – I-Feel-Anger
I'm-Beginning to Thirst – For-Human-Blood

(Repeat Chorus)

Awaken-With a Burning – In-My-Chest
Looking-Up – At a Man – With a Smoking-Gun
He's-Blessing-Me – With-Sadness – In-His-Eyes
Laughing – Gurgling-Blood – Complete-Circle is Here
My-Fate – As a Werewolf is Finally-Sealed – No-More
Blood-On-My-Tongue – No-Human-Meat – Inside-My-Belly
Now-I'm-Dead – No-More to Say – But – I-Was-Wolf
I Lived-It – My-Way – Is-That-The-Devil – I-See

(The Devil Speaks)
Come Here Wolfy Boy! – Ha, Ha, Ha, Ha – Burn Wolfy Boy Burn!

(Repeat Chorus)

19. Rip You Apart While Drinking You Down

Feast and Undead – With-Me
You-Shall-Live – For-Eternity
As-One of The – Night-Creatures
Nothing to Fear – Death's-Gone-Away
Leaving-You a Vampire – It-Will-Take
Awhile – Soon-You-Will-Feel – Blessed

Heaven or Hell – Right or Wrong
Means-Nothing – When-There-Is
Dripping-Crimson – In-The-Moonlight
Living-Off of Human-Blood
You-Will-Love – Our-Way to Their-End

Oh-What a Feeling – To-Be-Free – From-Sin
We've-Been-Damned – For so Long – That it Makes
No-Difference – We-Do – What-We-Do
No-Remorse – Just-Thrills and Blood

(Chorus)
There's Nothing You Can Do
So Give Yourselves To Us
It's Much Easier That Way – If You
Don't Do This – We'll Hunt You Down And
Rip You Apart While Drinking You Down

Humankind – Our-Prey – Our-Drink of Choice
For-You – Sometimes-Some-Lust – Enjoy-You-Will
Bleeding-For-Us – Enjoy-You-Will – Dying-For-Us
Stand-In-Line – If-You-Look-Tasty – We'll-Talk
No-Shame – Wanting-It – It's a Marvelous-Thing
No-Empty-Promises – We'll-Take-From-You – All-That-We-Want

We-Don't-Care – Leave-You-Alive or Dead – We-Won't-Stop-'Til
You-Start to Taste-Bad – Then-We'll-Throw-You-Away
Keep-On-Drinking – 'Cause-We're-Always-Thirsty – For-More-Blood

(Chorus)
There's Nothing You Can Do
So Give Yourselves To Us
It's Much Easier That Way – If You
Don't Do This – We'll Hunt You Down And
Rip You Apart While Drinking You Down

(This Song is for Entertainment Only. If you are Contemplating Suicide – Please-Tell-Someone or Get-Some-Help.)

20. Bleeding My Beast Blood Upon The Floor

(The Fool)
I-Have to Cut – The-Bad-Part – Out of Me
Let-It-Bleed – Upon-The-Floor
I-Am-Trash and Filth – I-Should-No-Longer-Exist
Death-I-Am – Calling to Thee
What-I've-Done – Over and Over
Who the Hell – Do-I – Think-I-Am
Just-Another – Worthless-Spit
Who-Was-Made – To-Like – Killing a Lot

The-Blood-Has-Permanently – Stained-My-Mind
Body and Soul – It is All-Gone – Finally – The-Blood
Doesn't-Want-Me-Anymore – Now-I'm-Useless – Worthless
I-Have to End – My-Existence – On-This-World of Rot

(Chorus #1)
Bleeding My Beast Blood Upon The Floor
It Is Done With Me – I Have To Give It Away
Bleeding My Beast Blood Upon The Floor
Who Is Ready – To Take My Place
Bleeding My Beast Blood Upon The Floor
Who Wants Evil Inside Them – That Makes Them Kill And Die

I-Cut-Myself-Hard – Deep and Fine
Bleeding-My-Beast-Blood – Upon-The-Floor
It-Will-Soak-In – Find-It's-Way-Up
To-Some-Other-Fool – That-Will-Do – Its-Bidding
Just-Because – It-Doesn't-Need-Me
Doesn't-Mean – That-It's-Over
It-Will-Flow-Through and Seep-Out
To-Find-Another – To-Rip – This-World-Apart

(Chorus #1)
Bleeding My Beast Blood Upon The Floor
It Is Done With Me And I Have To Give It Away
Bleeding My Beast Blood Upon The Floor
Who Is Ready To Take My Place
Bleeding My Beast Blood Upon The Floor
Who Wants Evil Inside Them – That Makes Them Kill And Die

(The Blood)
I'll-Seep-Out and Soak-In – I-Soak-In and Take-Over
In-You-I-Will-Be – Until-I-Make-You-Die – For-Me
All-For-Me – I-Am-The-Beast – You-Have to Worship-Me

You-Mean-Nothing – Just a Tool – To-Bring-Me – My-Meals
Feed-Me – Feed-Me – I-Am-Always-Hungry – Flesh and Blood
Oh-Yeah – Watch-Me – Look-At-My-Splendor – Watch-The-Flesh
Shred-In-My-Teeth – The-Blood-Flowing-Out – With-Every-Bite

(Chorus #2)
Bleed Your Beast Blood Upon The Floor
That's It My Tool – My Useless Fool
Bleed Your Beast Blood Upon The Floor
You're Weak And Your Soul Is Almost Dead
Bleed Your Beast Blood Upon The Floor
Last Drop Spilled – I'm Ready To Find Another Fool

Bleed-For-Me or Die – Don't-Matter – Be-My-Purpose
Do-You-Really – Have a Choice
Do-You-Really – Want a Choice
Naw-You-Love-Me – I-Am-The-Beast
I'm so Deliciously-Splendid – Now-Get-Up
Do-My-Bidding – I'm-Hungry-Again

I-Am-The-Beast
I-Am-Soaked – In-Your-Blood
I-Make-You-Taste – The-Blood of My-Victims
When-You-Feed-Me – 'Til-The-Day-You-Die
I-Am-The-Beast – Love – Worship and Feed-Me

I-Am – The-Original-Fear
I-Am – The-Original-Evil
I-Am-Eternal – I-Am-The-Beast
I-Am-The-First-Evil – I-Am-The-Beast

(Chorus #2)
Bleed Your Beast Blood Upon The Floor
That's It My Tool – My Useless Fool
Bleed Your Beast Blood Upon The Floor
You're Weak And Your Soul Is Almost Dead
Bleed Your Beast Blood Upon The Floor
Last Drop Spilled – I'm Ready To Find Another Fool

Here I Stand (841.)

Here-I-Stand – The-Last-Warrior
Damn-The-Rest – Survival-Was-The-Prize
Heaven or Hell – Is-There a Choice – But-One
War-Bloody-War – War-Bloody-War
I-Fought – I-Killed – I-Won – So-Many-Faces
In-My-Mind – Hate-My-Soul to Death
Too-Bad – So-Sad – Too-Bad – So-Sad
What-Can a Sexy – Male-Model-Do
But-Keep – Going-On and On
'Til-I – Get to Love-Bone – In-Heaven

(Chorus)
Here I Stand – The War Is Over
Here I Stand – Heaven Let Me In
Here I Stand – Why The Wait
Don't I Deserve My Wings
Here I Stand – I'm All Alone
Here I Stand – Heaven Ignores Me
Here I Stand – I Don't Like This
I Think I'm In A Lot Of Trouble

Here-I-Stand – The-Last-Warrior
Damn-The-Rest – Survival-Was-The-Prize
Heaven or Hell – Is-There a Choice – But-One
War-Bloody-War – War-Bloody-War
I-Fought – I-Killed – I-Won – So-Many-Faces
In-My-Mind – Hate-My-Soul to Death
Too-Bad – So-Sad – Too-Bad – So-Sad
What-Can a Sexy – Male-Model-Do
But-Keep – Going-On and On
'Til-I – Get to Love-Bone – In-Heaven

(Chorus)
Here I Stand – The War Is Over
Here I Stand – Heaven Let Me In
Here I Stand – Why The Wait
Don't I Deserve My Wings
Here I Stand – I'm All Alone
Here I Stand – Heaven Ignores Me
Here I Stand – I Don't Like This
I Think I'm In A Lot Of Trouble

Hello-Living-World of Humans
I-Sing-This to You – From-Hell
Good-News –For-You
Purgatory is Open-Again

Repent – You-Damned-Sinners
Pray – You-Heavenly-Believers
Your-Souls – Have a Second-Chance
All-Because-Of-Me – Kayden-Hart
Winner of The-War of Purgatory
New – Ruler of Hell

(Chorus)
Time After Time
Woman After Woman
Can You Believe It – Call Me A
Pretty Faced Bastard
After I Love Bone Them
Then Leave Them To Love-Bone Some More

Hell – Women-Are-Everywhere
Unfortunately – Most of Them – Are-Hags
Earth – I-Miss-You – Living-Ladies
That-Never-Said – No to Me
Heaven – Never-Been-There-Before
However – I've-Enjoyed the Taste
From-Having-Sex – With-Angels

Do-I-Piss-You-Off – Too-Damn-Bad
Like-I-Give a Hell – I'm-Damned
Love-Me or Hate-Me – Don't-Matter
I-Always-Find – Something to Love-Bone

(Chorus)
Time After Time
Woman After Woman
Can You Believe It – Call Me A
Pretty Faced Bastard
After I Love Bone Them
Then Leave Them To Love-Bone Some More

41

Speak As One (Original Version)

Come-On-Everybody
Stop-Being so Down
Time to Raise-Up – Some-Fire
The-Fire – That-Burns – Inside-Us-All
Know-Damn-Well – That-You-Feel-It
What-You – Gonna-Do-About- It
Just-Sit – Eat – Crap – Then-Repeat

No-Way-Man – I'm-Not-Down – With-That
I-Gotta-Be-Me – The-One and Only
Look at Me – With- Hate
It-Goes-Straight-Through
And-Leaves – No-Scars

You-Mean-Nothing to We-This-Way
Just a Big – Overfilled-Bag of Vile
Looking for Someone to Pop-It for You
So-You-Can – Give-Them-Everything
That-You-Have – Stored-Up
Well-Let-We – Tell-You-This

(Chorus)
Speak – Speak As One
They Have Nothing For That
Total Power Are We
When We Speak As One
Come Together Everybody
And Let's Speak As One

(Spoken)
Stop – Stop Man Stop – (Why?)
Man This Ain't Working – (Keep Going)
I Don't Think – (They'll Listen)
I Don't Know Man – (Be Positive)
Alright I'll Try – (Not Try, But Do it)
Don't Think They're Listening – (I Am)
So Just Speak To We – As We Was One – (You Got It)

Alright-Let's-Try – This-Again
We're-going to Speak as One
The-Time is Now to Speak as One

(Chorus)
Speak – Speak As One
They Have Nothing For That
Total Power Are We
When We Speak As One
Come Together Everybody
And Let's Speak As One

Don't-Matter – What-This-Time
The-System – Has to Bring – Us-Down
Don't-Matter – Who-We-Are
If-We're-Working or Poor
With-Shelter or Not – We're-All-Prey

Right-Wants-Us – To-Pray
Kneel-To-God's-Way
Pray-For-Everything
Left-Wants-Us – To-Bow
To-All-Their – Great-Power
Thankful-For-Everything

You-Know-What – I-Say-To-Both
No-Way-Man – Don't-Want-Either
Does-Not-Fit – My-Life-Style
Time-For-Both of You to Get
The-Hell – Out of The-Way
Of-Our – New-Day and Way
Because – If-You-Don't
We-Will-Never – Ascend
To-Our-Next-Phase

(Chorus)
Speak – Speak As One
They Have Nothing For That
Total Power Are We
When We Speak As One
Come Together Everybody
And Let's Speak As One

43

Anarchy-You-Scream – At-We
We-Are-Not-Listening – This-Time
We-Are-Not-Afraid – See-Us-Not-Shake
Revolution – The-Giants-Must-Fall
When-We – Speak-As-One
You-With-The – Power-Of-God
You-With-The – All-Power
Cannot-Touch-Us – Anymore
Our-Eyes – Are-20/20
We-Can-Hear – The-Needle – When-Dropped

You-Bring-Your-Bibles and War-Machines
We'll-Bring – Only-Ourselves
We-Will-Make – Our-Stand
No-More of This-Crap
We-Are-Going to Make – This-Country-Stop
Make-You – Taste-Reality

You-Are – The-Nothing
We-Are-The-Power – See-You-Shake
You-Can't-Believe – This-Is-Happening
We-Can – We-Have-No-Doubt
We-Speak – As-One
Millions-Of-Us – As-One
What-Did-You-Think – Would-Happen

(Chorus)
Speak – Speak As One
They Have Nothing For That
Total Power Are We
When We Speak As One
Come Together Everybody
And Let's Speak As One

(Spoken)
What Do You Think Man? – (Great)
Naw Really? – (Damn Great)
Think So Do You Man? – (Yeah, I Do)
Will It Get Through Or Will This Be For Nothing?
(I'm With You I Feel Empowered)
Thanks Man – I Feel Like Leaving Now
(Later This Was Great) – You Take It Easy Man

The Invention Of Mind Rockin'

I've always been a fan of music, classic rock, rock and roll, hard rock and heavy metal. I've also always been a fan of movies, comedy drama, action, suspense, fantasy and horror. As a kid my hobby was writing lyrics that I created in my mind. In 2013 I took my hobby, my passion for music and movies and with them I created Mind Rockin'. By doing so I made myself become something that I never thought or dreamed of doing before and that was to become a self-published author. My creation of Mind Rockin' works like this. I sit down in front of my computer and come up with a melody or score in my mind to go along with the original songs or lyrical stories that I am creating. However when you the reader/singer reads or sings the song or lyrical story, there is no right or wrong for the melody or score that you come up with in your minds, be it rock and roll, pop, country or rap. Mind Rockin' is a concept I created for persons just like myself, those of us that would like to be able to do or create something like stories or songs but with no opportunity knocking at the door this dream of ours stays that, a dream. Mind Rockin' is the only thing in the world where the person you are has the chance to use what's inside you instead of the usual way where it is only one way for everybody, and that is the way the creator intended for it to be foretold or heard.

I'd like to dedicate this book and thank my Wife of Twenty-Four years, I love you Christina thank you for your Love and Support.

I'd like to thank all my Family and all my Friends. Thank you to all my Fans, I am a Fan of yours as well, together We can make a difference. Let's Shout It Out and Speak As One.

The Gemini Rising Rockin' Machine.

Publication Dates (Original Versions)

Book One:
Who Am I?
October 11, 2013

Book Two:
Mind Rockin'
May 01, 2014

Book Three:
Big Time Love
July 20, 2014

Book Four:
Love High
July 20, 2014

Purgatory's Full:
A Song, A Dream Or A Cold Hard Reality In Thirty-Six Parts
July 20, 2014

Book Six:
Do You Remember Rock And Roll?
September 18, 2014

Book Seven:
Rock And Roll Bachelor
September 18, 2014

Book Five:
Siphon Your Minds &
The Vegetarian And The Slaughterhouse
October 27, 2014

Book Eight:
The End & An Ordinary Day In Hell
November 20, 2014

THE GEMINI RISING ROCKIN' MACHINE

BOOK TWO: MIND ROCKIN'

Book Two: Mind Rockin'
Copyright 2016 by The Gemini Rising Rockin' Machine

ISBN-13: 978-0692210604 (Gemini Rising Rockin' Machine,The)
ISBN-10: 0692210601

For questions, comments you may send correspondence to.

thegeminirisingrockinmachine@twc.com

Official Website
www.thegeminirisingrockinmachine.com

BOOK TWO: MIND ROCKIN' (Pages 48-96)

(Synopsis)

(SIDE ONE)
Mind Rockin': Don't need anyone you can do it yourself.
Thickness of Mind: Clearly thinking now.
Stranger Calling No One: The Last man on Earth?.
The Last Rocker: No one needs him anymore.
Dying While Texting: Stop it and live.

(SIDE TWO)
I Love You: Last days he has left and she is the only one that matters.
Darken Our Love: Wants a second chance.
Break Me When You're Done With Me: Forgets to remove Her tag.
Through the Flame of a Candle: He keeps Evil at bay.
Tapped: Being checked on.

(SIDE THREE)
We Are Here: A force of power.
The Church of No God: A church of human power.
Pets and Monsters: Why do so many of them get mistreated?
Justice: Drunk driver, dead little girl, Justice?
3 Can Corn Man: Big bad man VS Three Terrorist

(SIDE FOUR)
Empty Hands: And he needs to fill them.
Evil Pill: Do you believe him?.
Bam Burn Dead Hell: Three Different events that tie in together.
I. The Sighting   II. The Vision
III. Future Burning People of This Earth
Freaking Zombies Man: What a end to a blind date.
Set Loose on Hell: One more thing to do.

The numbers after the song titles are the original numbering.

(SIDE ONE)
21. Mind Rockin' (122.)
22. Thickness Of Mind (72.)
23. Stranger Calling No One (81.)
24. The Last Rocker (98.)
25. Dying While Texting (105.)
    Dying While Texting (Original Version)

(SIDE TWO)
26. I Love You (87.)
27. Darken Our Love (38.)
28. Break Me When You're Done With Me (96.)
29. Through the Flame Of A Candle (86.)
30. Tapped (76.)

(SIDE THREE)
   I'm Number, It Don't Matter **(801.)** (New Cover Bonus)
31. We Are Here (64.)
32. The Church Of No God (65.)
33. Pets And Monsters (126.)
34. Justice (05.)
    Justice (2.0 Version) **(687.)**
35. 3 Can Corn Man (111.)

(SIDE FOUR)
   Yesterday Was Not So Great **(806.)** (New Cover Bonus)
36. Empty Hands (23.)
37. Evil Pill (113.)
38. Bam Burn Dead Hell (61.)
I. The Sighting II. The Vision III. Future Burning People Of This Earth
39. Freaking Zombies Man (84.)
40. Set Loose On Hell (83.)

Rock Don't Hurt **(622.)** (New Cover Bonus)
Rock Fever (Can You Feel It) **(750.)** (New Cover Bonus)
The Last Rocker #2 **(586.)** (New Cover Bonus)
The Last Rocker #3 **(588.)** (New Cover Bonus)
We Are Here (Original Version)

21. Mind Rockin'

It's-Not-For-Sale – At-Any-Price – But-It's-Totally-Free
Reach-In-Deep – Pull-Something-Out – That-Is-Exclusive
To-You – Come-On-Everybody – Let's-Do-Some-Mind-Rockin'

Who-Am-I – Do-You-Know
Do-I-Really – Want-You-To-Tell-Me
Am-I-Better-Off – Not Knowing – Who Am I

I'm-The-Man – That-Has-No-Past – Laughing-At-Nothing
While-Nothing-Is-Funny – Who-Am-I
Can't-Even-Remember – The-Dreams – That-Wake
Me-Screaming – Please-Tell-Me – Who-I-Am

It's-Not-For-Sale – At-Any-Price – But-It's-Totally-Free
Reach-In-Deep – Pull-Something-Out – That-Is-Exclusive
To-You – Come-On-Everybody – Let's-Do-Some-Mind-Rockin'

Hello, Are-You-In-There – Can-You-Make-It – Out-Of-There
Your-Mind-Is-Melting – Can't-You-Feel-It – You're-Drifting-Away
Can-I-Help-You – Yes-I-Can – However – I'm-All-In-Your-Mind

(Chorus)
Grabbed My Lazy Mind
And For The Very First Time
I Created – Mind Rockin'
Made All The Jumbling – Slow Down
As My Mind-Full Of Thick Haze
Expelled From Way Down Inside Me
Like It Was A Bad Trip – That Has Lasted For Years

As-Time – Went-By-Slowly
My-Down – Playing-Mind
Got-Stuck – In-Some-Mind-Funk
Living-Day-To-Day
Like-It-Was-Yesterday

Things-Happened – Things-Changed
As-My-Mind – Kept-Slipping-Away
On-A-Downward-Spiral
That-I-Did-Not – Pay-Attention-To
Until-One-Night – I-Did

Do-You-Remember – Rock-And-Roll
And-What-It-Did
For-You-And-Your-Soul
It-Kept-You-Young – Free-And-Hard
So-Come-Back-To-Rock
Start-Rocking – And-Rolling-Again

Rock-Rock – Rock-And-Roll-House
Rock-Rock – It's-A-Rock-And-Roll-House

(Chorus)
Grabbed My Lazy Mind
And For The Very First Time
I Created – Mind Rockin'
Made All The Jumbling – Slow Down
As My Mind-Full Of Thick Haze
Expelled From Way Down Inside Me
Like It Was A Bad Trip – That Has Lasted For Years

Can-I – Ask-You-This
Why-The-Hell-Does
Rock-Seem-Dead
It-Was-Everywhere-Once
Making-This-Planet-Seem-Better
I-Don't-Know – About-You
But-I – Sure As Hell – Miss It

Rock-Seems-Dead
Mother-Earth – Is-Crying
Rock-Seems-Dead
All-The-People – Are-Dying
Rock-Seems-Dead
This-Seems – So-Familiar
Rock-Seems-Dead
I-Think – I'm-Having – A-Flash-Back

Rock-Seems-Dead
Maybe-It's-All – In-My-Mind
Rock-Seems-Dead
Maybe-It's-Not – In-My-Mind
Rock-Seems-Dead
This-Seems – So-Familiar
Rock-Seems-Dead
I-Think – I'm-Having – A-Flash-Back
51

(Chorus)
Grabbed My Lazy Mind
And For The Very First Time
I Created – Mind Rockin'
Made All The Jumbling – Slow Down
As My Mind-Full Of Thick Haze
Expelled From Way Down Inside Me
Like It Was A Bad Trip – That Has Lasted For Years

Memories-Of-Long-Ago – In-My-Mind
Calling-Me-Back – Through-Time
To-Forget – All-My-Heavies
To-Party-Hardy – And-Rock-On
Like-My-Life – Is-On-The-Line

I-Remember – Rock-And-Roll
And-What-It-Did – For-My-Mind
I-Remember – Rock-And-Roll
It-Kept-Me – Young-And-Free
I-Remember – Rock-And-Roll
Like-A-Yesterday's – Dream-Come-True
I-Remember – Rock-And-Roll
So-I'm-Going-To-Start
Rock-And-Rolling-Again
'Til-The-Day – I-Die

Rock-Rock – Rock-And-Roll-House
Rock-Rock – It's-A-Rock-And-Roll-House
Rock-Rock – Rock-And-Roll-House
Rock-Rock – It's-A-Rock-And-Roll-House

(Chorus)
Grabbed My Lazy Mind
And For The Very First Time
I Created – Mind Rockin'
Made All The Jumbling – Slow Down
As My Mind-Full Of Thick Haze
Expelled From Way Down Inside Me
Like It Was A Bad Trip – That Has Lasted For Years

Time-Goes-By-So-Fast – Tomorrow-Is-Not
Yesterday-Anymore – As-Today-Always-Brings
Something-New – For-My-Mind-Rockin' – Mind-To
Discover-And-Change-Into – Songs-And-Lyrical-Stories

Soft-To-Hard – Hard-To-Soft – Sunshine-And-Snowdrifts
Ready-To-Bask-Me – In-Warmth – Ready-To-Freeze-Me – Frozen
It's-All-Spinning – Within-My-Mind – Just-Like-Before
Only-Now – I'm-Almost-In – Full-Control
As-I-Pick-Out – From-The-Forever – Pool-Of-Thoughts
Something-That-Smiles or Something-That-Bleeds

(Chorus)
Grabbed My Lazy Mind
And For The Very First Time
I Created – Mind Rockin'
Made All The Jumbling – Slow Down
As My Mind-Full Of Thick Haze
Expelled From Way Down Inside Me
Like It Was A Bad Trip – That Has Lasted For Years

It's-Not-For-Sale – At-Any-Price – But-It's-Totally-Free
Reach-In-Deep – Pull-Something-Out – That-Is-Exclusive
To-You – Come-On-Everybody – Let's-Do-Some-Mind-Rockin'

Who-Am-I – Do-You-Know
Do-I-Really – Want-You-To-Tell-Me
Am-I-Better-Off – Not Knowing – Who Am I

I'm-The-Man – That-Has-No-Past – Laughing-At-Nothing
While-Nothing-Is-Funny – Who-Am-I
Can't-Even-Remember – The-Dreams – That-Wake
Me-Screaming – Please-Tell-Me – Who-I-Am

It's-Not-For-Sale – At-Any-Price – But-It's-Totally-Free
Reach-In-Deep – Pull-Something-Out – That-Is-Exclusive
To-You – Come-On-Everybody – Let's-Do-Some-Mind-Rockin'

(Chorus)
Grabbed My Lazy Mind
And For The Very First Time
I Created – Mind Rockin'
Made All The Jumbling – Slow Down
As My Mind-Full Of Thick Haze
Expelled From Way Down Inside Me
Like It Was A Bad Trip – That Has Lasted For Years

Rock-Rock – Rock-And-Roll-House
Rock-Rock – It's-A-Rock-And-Roll-House
53

22. Thickness Of Mind

Time's-Slipped-Away
I-Did-Not – Pay-Attention to It
For-Every-Day – Was the Same – I-Just
Lived-Them – One-Day – At a Time

My-Mind – Would-Have – Kept-Slipping
Down the Thickness – Of a Mind-Spiral
If-Not-For – Mind-Rockin'
It-Was-The-Jolt – My-Mind-Craved

Waiting is Not – For-Me-Anymore
Now-That-I've – Caught-Back-Up
With-My-Mind – Now-I'm-Ready
Now-I'm-Eager – To-Take-My-Chance

(Chorus)
A Feeling Of Thickness Has Left
My Mind – Clarity Has Surfaced
I'm Alright Again – Free To Take
My Chance Now – Since My
Thickness Of Mind – Has Went Away

Everyday-My-Mind – Becomes-Stronger
Time is Still – Slipping-By
Has-My-Chance – Came and Went
Seems to Be – My-Chance
Is a Slow – Work-In-Progress

This-Does-Not – Matter
I-Will-Not-Stop – Until-I-Make-It
Even-If-I-Get – Chance-Blocked
Mind-Rockin' – Will-Keep-My-Mind – Free and Ready
For-When-The-World – Is-Ready-For-We

(Chorus)
A Feeling Of Thickness Has Left
My Mind – Clarity Has Surfaced
I'm Alright Again – Free To Take
My Chance Now – Since My
Thickness Of Mind – Has Went Away

23. A Stranger Calling No One

Is-There – Anyone-Out-There
It's-Been – So-Long – Too-Long
Since-I've-Felt – Anyone-Around
Just-Day – After-Day of Silence
I-Am – All-Alone
Don't-Know – For-How-Long
Didn't-Think to Keep-Track
I-Don't-Think – It-Makes a Difference
When-Every-Day is The-Same

(Chorus)
I Am Calling Out To You
But I Never Get An Answer
It Seems I Have Become
A Stranger Calling No One

I've-Tried-Not – Talking to Myself
The-Loneliness – Compels-Me-To
Have a Bad-Feeling – If-I-Don't
I'll-Lose – My-Humanity
Days-Out – Looking-For-Anyone
Never-Did-Any-Good – Always-The-Same
Every-Direction – Only-More-Destruction
More-Rubble for Me to Shift-Through
I-Can't-Afford to Keep on Hurting-Myself

(Chorus)
I Am Calling Out To You
But I Never Get An Answer
It Seems I Have Become
A Stranger Calling No One

Why-The-Hell – Am-I the Only-One
What-The-Hell – Happened
Didn't – Anyone – Survive
If-They-Did – Where-The-Hell – They-At
No-This-Can-Not-Be – Makes-No-Damn-Sense
There-Has to Be – More-Than-Me
I-Cannot – Create-Life by Myself
For-I-Am – Only-One-Man

(Repeat chorus)
55

24. The Last Rocker

With-Guitar – Over-My-Shoulder
I-Still-Walk – The-Highways
Trying to Find a Gig – It's-Hard on My-Mind
I-Will-Continue-On – I'm a Rocker

On-Stage is My-Home – I'm-Free
In-Front of A-Crowd – Playing-My-Guitar
Singing-From – Within-My-Soul
I-Bleed-Pure – Rock and Roll

(Chorus)
Nobody Wants To Hear My Songs
This Singing – Guitar Playing Nomad
Has No One To Play For
Without Noticing It I've Become
The Last Rocker

Nobody Wants To Hear My Songs
This Singing – Guitar Playing Nomad
Has No One To Play For
Without Noticing It I've Become
The Last Rocker

Made so Many-People – Feel-Good
Rockin'-Along to My-Songs
Year-After-Year – Band-After-Band
I've-Traveled-On – Living-The-Life

Busted-For-Rocking – Too-Hard
My-Fans-Cheering – While-Others-Hissing
I-Kicked-Ass – I-Got-Laid-Lots
I-Was-Loved – I-Was-Hated
I-Will-Continue-On – I'm a Rocker

(Chorus)
Nobody Wants To Hear My Songs
This Singing – Guitar Playing Nomad
Has No One To Play For
Without Noticing It I've Become
The Last Rocker

56

Nobody-Stops and Picks-Me-Up
I'm a Past – Best-Forgotten-About
I-Still-Walk – The-Streets and Highways
Trying to Find a Gig – It's-Hard on My-Soul
I-Will-Continue-On – I'm a Rocker

I've-Been-Beaten-Up – Robbed-Many-Times
I'm-Trying to Find a Music-Store
To-Fix-My-Guitar – That-Was-Kicked-Around
I-Was-Bloody – They-Just-Left-Me
In-The-Middle of The-Street – Like-Trash

(Chorus)
Nobody Wants To Hear My Songs
This Singing – Guitar Playing Nomad
Has No One To Play For
Without Noticing It I've Become
The Last Rocker

It's-Been-Years-Now – Rock and Roll
Is-Dead – No-More-Music-Stores
No-More-Record-Shops – People-Playing-Music
All-The-Music – Around-The-World
Has-Silently – Disappeared

No-One-Remembers – What's-The-Point
Why-Go-On – Think-I'll-Find a Nice
Quiet-Place and Fade-Away
Maybe-Go to Rock-N-Roll – Heaven
Maybe-Go to Rock-N-Roll – Hell

(Chorus)
Nobody Wants To Hear My Songs
This Singing – Guitar Playing Nomad
Has No One To Play For
Without Noticing It I've Become
The Last Rocker

Nobody Wants To Hear My Songs
This Singing – Guitar Playing Nomad
Has No One To Play For
Without Noticing It I've Become
The Last Rocker

25. Dying While Texting

Friday-Night – Party-Time
Driving – Passing-The-Time
Dudes and I – Can't-Wait to Get-Laid
Tonight – Going-To a Big-Party
Going to Meet – Our-Ladies-There
Beer – Locked-Up – In-The-Trunk
No-Worries – In-Sight

(Chorus)
Hey Dumb Asses – Yeah
You're In Love – So The Hell What
Put The Phone To Your Ears You Idiot Holes
While Driving In Your Rolling Death Machines
Stop Doing This You Horny Fools
Maybe You'll Live To Get You Some
Instead Of Dying While Texting

Having a Great-Time – Everybody is Pumped
Have to Text – My-Little-Lady
Tell-Her – I'm-On-My-Way – BTS
Look-Up – From-My-Phone – Too-Late
My-Light is Red – Wrecker's-Light is Green
No-Time to Stop – We're-Going to Die

(Chorus)
Hey Dumb Asses – Yeah
You're In Love – So The Hell What
Put The Phone To Your Ears You Idiot Holes
While Driving In Your Rolling Death Machines
Stop Doing This You Horny Fools
Maybe You'll Live To Get You Some
Instead Of Dying While Texting

(Spoken)
Party-Car – Crashes-Into a Wrecker – Crunching
Party-Car – All-The-Way to The-Back-Seat
Everybody-Dies – Very-Bloodily
Silently and Screaming – Into-The-Night

All-The-Phones – Survived-The-Crash
And-All – Were-Given to Charity

58

Dying While Texting (Original Version)

Driving – Having-Some-Fun
Friday – Triple-Date-Night
Picked-My-Boys and Their-Chicks-Up

Now-It's-Time to Pick-Up-My-Babe
Think-I'll – Send-Her a Text
Bet-She's-Home – Getting-All-Sexy

Love-The-Way – She-Smiles at Me
When-I-Tell-Her – How-Hot-She-Looks
Grabbing-Her-Up – For a Hug
Feeling-Her-Melt – In-My-Arms
While-I-Kiss-Her – Like-I'm-The-Man

(Chorus)
Hey Dumb Asses – Yeah
You're In Love – So The Hell What
Put The Phone To Your Ears – You Idiot Holes
While Driving In Your – Rolling Death Machines
Start Doing This – You Horny Fools
Maybe You'll Live – To Get You Some
Instead Of Dying While Texting

Having a Great-Time – Everybody is Pumped
Have to Text – My-Little-Lady
Tell-Her – I'm-On-My-Way

Damn – Dropped-The-Phone
Sorry-Folks – Car-Has-The-Shakes
BTS

Looking-Up – From-My-Phone – Too-Late
My-Light is Red – Wrecker's-Light is Green
No-Time to Stop – We're-Going to Die

(Spoken)
Party-Car – Crashes-Into a Wrecker – Crunching
Party-Car – All-The-Way to The-Back-Seat
Everybody-Dies – Very-Bloodily
Silently and Screaming – Into-The-Night

59

(Chorus)
Hey Dumb Asses – Yeah
You're In Love – So The Hell What
Put The Phone To Your Ears – You Idiot Holes
While Driving In Your – Rolling Death Machines
Start Doing This – You Horny Fools
Maybe You'll Live – To Get You Some
Instead Of Dying While Texting

(Spoken)
She-Sits and Waits – Looking – All-Friday-Night

Getting-Bored – Thirty-Minutes-Now
What-They-Do – Go to Dinner – Without-Me
There's a Light – In the Drive-Way – Yep-That's-Them

Steve-You're so Lucky to Have-Me
We're-Going to Do a Little-Talking
About-Keeping – Me-Waiting
Damn-Not-Them – Where-The-Hell-Are-They

Think-I'll-Send – Him a Text
Tired of Waiting
Want to Have – Some-Fun
It's-Friday-Night – After-All

(Chorus)
Hey Dumb Asses – Yeah
You're In Love – So The Hell What
Put The Phone To Your Ears – You Idiot Holes
While Driving In Your – Rolling Death Machines
Start Doing This – You Horny Fools
Maybe You'll Live – To Get You Some
Instead Of Dying While Texting

(Spoken)
All-Phones – Survived-The-Crash
And-All-Were – Given to Charity

26. I Love You

I-Come-Home to You
My-Best-Friend – My-Wife
Telling-You of My-Sadness
You're – Not – There
Still-Out – Doing-Your-Things

Now-That – I'm-Alone
I'm-Thinking – I-Should-Wait
Let-Us-Have – One-Good-Night
Before-Our-Lives – Change

(Chorus)
I Love You
I've Been So Happy With You
All The Love We Shared
For All These Wonderful Years
Don't Even Remember A Bad Time Now
All I Know Is That I Love You

My-Love – Don't-Have-Much-Time-Left
Ugly-Has – Gotten-Inside-Me
Ugly-Will be Taking – My-Life-Away
Doctor-Told-Me to Get-Myself in Order

I-Know-You-Love-Me – You-Don't-Want-This
This is Happening-Baby – We-Can't-Change-This
Let's-Live the Life – We-Would-Have-Lived
In-The-Few-Days – That-I-Have-Left

(Chorus)
I Love You
I've Been So Happy With You
All The Love We Shared
For All These Wonderful Years
Don't Even Remember A Bad Time Now
All I Know Is That I Love You

You-Buried-Me – On a Rainy-Day
Your-Tears – Mixed-With-The-Rain
You-Feel-Like – You've-Also-Died
In-Time-My-Love – You'll-Find-Love
Open-Your-Heart – When-It's-Healed

27. Darken Our Love

I-Never – Loved-You – More-Than
When-I-Needed-You – The-Most
Your-Body – Kept-Me-Strong
Your-Love – Kept-Me-Solid

Then-One-Night – Mr.-Love-Bone
Wanted-Some-Stray – I-Said-Yes
To-My-Surprise – She-Knows-You
She-Hates-You – She-Used-Me
Just to Tell-You – This

(Chorus)
Oh Babe – Can't You Feel It
I Love You – So Much
I Want To Feel – Your Touch
You Mean – Everything To Me
Please Forgive Me – I Am
So Sorry – Sweet Baby
That I – Darken Our Love

I-Took-Advantage of You and Your
Love-Baby – You-Were-My-One
She-Means-Nothing to Me-Baby
Just-An-Itch – That-Needed to Be-Scratched

She's-Over and Gone-Baby
I'm-Done and Bored – So-Baby
Forgive-Me and Let's-Get-It-On
It's-Kinda – Your-Fault – Baby
For-Not – Telling-Me – About-Her

(Chorus)
Oh Babe – Can't You Feel It
I Love You – So Much
I Want To Feel – Your Touch
You Mean – Everything To Me
Please Forgive Me – I Am
So Sorry – Sweet Baby
That I – Darken Our Love

That's-Alright-Baby – I-Forgive-You
Now-Let's-Get-To – Having-Some-Sexy-Fun

28. Break Me When You're Done With Me

Time and Time – I-Have-Tried
To-Find – That-Special-Person
That-Wants to Give-Me – Their-Love
And-Take-Mine – In-Return
I've-Tried – So-Hard – Being-Someone
I-Think – They-Want
Erasing-What – Makes-Me – Me
And-All-They-Do – Is-Use – Then-Break-Me

(Chorus)
I Guess – I Forgot To Remove
My Tag – That Reads
Break Me When You're Done With Me
I Wish – I Would Remember
This Seems To Happen – Every Time
And I Am Tired – Of Being Broken

We-Met – On a Friday-Night
Everything-Was-Going – Too-Right
As-Our-Feelings and Passions-Grew
It-Was-Love – At-First-Sight – Before
I-Even-Knew-It – You-Were-Gone
You-Were-Lost – Nowhere to Be-Found

(Chorus)
I Guess – I Forgot To Remove
My Tag – That Reads
Break Me When You're Done With Me
I Wish – I Would Remember
This Seems To Happen – Every Time
And I Am Tired – Of Being Broken

Starting-Over – Without-You
Makes-Me – Lonely and Blue
You-Didn't – Leave a Note
You-Didn't – Leave a Clue
Now-My-Heart – Is-Broken-In-Two
Sadly-It-Seems – You're-Just – Like-The-Rest

(Repeat Chorus)

29. Through The Flame Of A Candle

Force of Power – God – Creates-First-Life
First-Came-Adam – Then-Came-Eve – I-Was #665
I-Am-The-Light-Keeper – This-I-Did-Not-Know
Men and Women – Everywhere – Living-Together
With-No-Hate – Inside-Themselves – Just-Lots of Love

I-Was-Created – Differently – Lived-My-Life
Did-Not-Know – or – Think of Why – I-Was-Alive
Everybody-Else-Was-Created – Paired-Up
Receive-Their-Callings – Walked-Off-Together
Did-Whatever – Needed to Be-Done
I-Watched and Waited – Patiently – For a Mate
To be Created – For-Me – For-I'm-Last to Be-Created

(Chorus)
Through The Flame Of A Candle
I Keep Evil At Bay
Forever And Always
For I Am The Light Keeper
Keeping Humanity Safe
From The Darkness Of Evil
That Infects And Kills Their Souls

First-Life – Stayed-The-Same – Until-The-Night
Adam and Eve – Became a New-Type of Being
Called-Human – They-Shared-Bodies – Everyone
Came to Watch – This-Happen – I-Did-Not-Know
What-This-Was-Called – or – Understand-Its-Meaning – But
Adam and Eve – Seemed to Enjoy-Themselves – Very-Much

Then-Out of Nowhere a Roar – In-The-Night-Sky
I-Looked-Up-Seeing – Nasty-Looking-Things – Ready to
Descend-Down-Upon – Adam and Eve – For-Creating-Life
Finally-I-Received – My-Calling – I-Knew-Instantly
They-Were-Evil – #666 To-Be-Created – They-Came-From-Hell
Sadness as Lucifer's – Golden-Wings – Turned to Black and White

Power of Light – Filled-My-Being – Giving-Me a Weapon
That-Is a Piece of Heaven's – Light – A-Candle
Appeared in My-Hand – I-Held it Up to The-Sky – The-Evil
Satan-Hissed in Fear – Then-Flew-Away – Back to Hell

(Chorus)
Through The Flame Of A Candle
I Keep Evil At Bay
Forever And Always
For I Am The Light Keeper
Keeping Humanity Safe
From The Darkness Of Evil
That Infects And Kills Their Souls

Day-One-Came – I'm-The-Light-Keeper of Heaven
All-First-Life-Changed – They-Were-Given-Souls
They-Lived-Short-Lives – Then-They-Died – Becoming-Angels
I-Live-Forever – I-Have-No-Soul – No-Heaven
Turned-Out – Lucifer and I – Were-The-Only-Ones
That-Were – Truly-Different – Never a Mate for Me
I'm to Be – Only-One – Forevermore

Year-After-Year – Uncalled for Evil – Tries to Enter-Earth
I-Sense-Their-Arrival – I-Soar to Them – Give-Them
No-Quarter – When-I-Pull-Out – My-Heaven's-Candle – and
Burn-Their-Nasty – Demon-Bodies – With-Heaven's-Light
They-Scream – I-Smile – They-Burn – I-Laugh – Sometimes
Satan-Appears and Roars – Out-Hell to Me – Like-He-Matters

(Chorus)
Through The Flame Of A Candle
I Keep Evil At Bay
Forever And Always
For I Am The Light Keeper
Keeping Humanity Safe
From The Darkness Of Evil
That Infects And Kills Their Souls

My-Calling is Simple – Keep-Evil at Bay
So-They-Cannot-Come of Their-Own-Free-Will
It is Hard on Me – Watching-One-After-Another
Of-The-Evil – That-Are-Allowed to Get-Through
I-Cannot-Stop-Them – They-Are-Called-For
Allowed to Spread – Their-Evil to The-Ones
That-Have a Need or A-Want-For-It

(Repeat Chorus)

65

30. Tapped

No-Crap – I'm-Telling-You – I-See-Angels-Now
They-Do-Not-Like-It – They-Do-Not-Like-Me
I-Was-Being – Tapped
First-Time – I-Saw an Angel
It-Was-Siphoning – My-Thoughts
Calculating-The-Good and The-Bad

Waking-Up – Seeing-This-Happening – I-Was-Frozen
As-It-Hissed and Flew-Away – Mad-I-Was-Seeing-It
Told-Me-This – With-Anger in Its-Voice
Brought-Down an Archangel – To-Get-Rid of Me
Ferocious as Can-Be – Hitting-Me – With-Everything it Had
Nothing-No-Pain – Its-Hits-Did-Not – Leave a Mark
Both-Angels-Cursed-Me – Then-Flew – Through-My-Wall

(Chorus)
Tapped
God's Workers Are So Busy
Sticking In Their Talon
To Find Out What I Have Done
My Mind Is Theirs Just To Tap Away

Being-Tapped is God's-Way of Finding-Out
His-Workers – Bring-Back the Information
Feed-It to The-Big – Machine-In-The-Sky
If-Any-Bells-Ring – They-Stop and Mark-It-Down
Pluses and Minuses – Good-Deeds and Our-Sins

None of You – Will-Ever-Know-This – Keep-Sleeping-Away
My-Blood-Condition and My-New-Pill – Have-Made-Me-Different
Found-Out – That-God-Does-Not-Know – All-About-Us
Until-He is Informed – By-The-Tapping of Us – I-Wonder
If-Some of Us – Do so Bad – So-Much-Wrong-Doing
That-There is No-Need – For-Us to Be – Ever-Tapped-Again

(Chorus)
Tapped
God's Workers Are So Busy
Sticking In Their Talon
To Find Out What I Have Done
My Mind Is Theirs Just To Tap Away

I'm Number, It Don't Matter (801.)

I'll-Try a Little-Harder
Dirty-Are – My-Hands and Feet
What-Can-I-Say – My-Life
Has-Scarred – My-Soul

Wake-Up – Wake-Up
World – Commands and Demands
Even-Though – It-Has-No – Use for I
Have to Keep on Showing – My-Face
No-Matter – What-I-Want

(Chorus)
My Number Is Showing
I'm Number, It Don't Matter
My Face And Soul – Don't Register
To The Great Big – Machine In The Sky
My Number Is Showing
I'm Number, It Don't Matter
Don't Be Like I
Live Your Life Free And Fine

I'll-Try a Little-Harder
Dirty-Are – My-Hands and Feet
What-Can-I-Say – My-Life
Has-Scarred – My-Soul

Hold-On – Hold -On
Number – It-Don't-Matter to Us
Stop – Where-You-Are – Right-Now
Remember – Before-You-Die
Perhaps-Tomorrow – You-Have-Enough
To-Pay – For-Your-Death

(Chorus)
My Number Is Showing
I'm Number, It Don't Matter
My Face And Soul – Don't Register
To The Great Big – Machine In The Sky
My Number Is Showing
I'm Number, It Don't Matter
Don't Be Like I And We
Live Your Life To The Fullest
67

31. We Are Here

We-Bleed and We-Bleed
We're-The-Children of Earth
With-No-Where to Run – In-The-End
When-Death – Comes-Knocking
With-Killing-Death – In-His-Hands
Play-Time and Death-Time
Which-One is Around-The-Corner
For-We to Welcome or Hide-From
It's-Not-Hard to Comprehend
Death is Killing-We – In-Every-Way

(Chorus)
We Are Here – We Are Here
We Want To Be Truly Free
But We Are Tied To This World
Stop Making So Much Killing Things
Start Make Living Things
We Are Here – We Are Here
No More Poison Waters And Lands
It Is Time To Take The Ugly Out
And Bring The Beauty Back In

No-More – Killing-Death – For-The-Answer
We're-Tired of Feeling – Pain and Fear
Let-Love – Come-Shining-Through
People of Wanting – Death and Torture
Even-With – All-Your-Souls – You-Still-Suck
We-Don't-Pray – Any-More – Why-Can't-You
Maybe-If-You – Stopped-Wanting – Heaven and Hell
You-Can-Live – In-Harmony – Like-The-Rest of We

(Chorus)
We Are Here – We Are Here
We Want To Be Truly Free
But We Are Tied To This World
Stop Making So Much Killing Things
Start Make Living Things
We Are Here – We Are Here
No More Poison Waters And Lands
It Is Time To Take The Ugly Out
And Bring The Beauty Back In

32. The Church Of No God

We-Are – We-Are – The-Church of No-God
We-Are – We-Are – The-Church of No-God
We-Are-Here – Not to Pray – For-The-Way
Do-You-Hear-Us – We-Don't-Fear-You – Your-Old
Faith of Hate and Ignorance – Is-Not – Welcomed-Here
Our-Church is Pure – Human-Power of Force

(Chorus)
It Don't Matter Who You Are
Where You Come From
Where You're Going
Just Come On In And Enjoy
The Glory Of The Day
No Dread Coming Down On You
Just The Embrace Of Humankind
You'll Feel The Difference
Of The Church Of No God

We-Are – We-Are – The-Church of No-God
We-Are – We-Are – The-Church of No-God
Get-Use to It – We-Are-Here to Stay
Can-You-See-Us – We-Don't-Fear-You
You-Fear-Us – How-Can-We – Be-This-Way

What-Can-We-Say – You'll-Never-Accept
The-Awakening-We-Had – Was-More-Powerful
Then-Your – Unreal-God's – Could-Ever-Give-You
We-Are-Sad – Maybe-Pleased to Say – You'll-Never-Find
True-Peace – You'll-Have to Stand and Stare
While-We-Grow and Rise-In-Delight – Loving-Our-Lives

(Chorus)
It Don't Matter Who You Are
Where You Come From
Where You're Going
Just Come On In And Enjoy
The Glory Of The Day
No Dread Coming Down On You
Just The Embrace Of Humankind
You'll Feel The Difference
Of The Church Of No God

33. Pets And Monsters

I'm-Barely-Alive – Almost-Dead
And-I-Hardly – Ever-Get-Fed
Beaten a Lot – Locked-In-Chains

I-Can-Not-Help – Liking to Bark
It's-So-Hot – I-Would-Love a Drink
But-I-Can't – Reach-My-Water

(Chorus)
I Was Suppose To Be
Your Best Friend
But A Human – Monster
Like You Is So Inhuman
Because You Can't Love
Even A Good – Dog Like Me

Master's-Home – Kinda-Early
Better-Put – My-Head
Down in Submission
He's-Such a Human – Monster
Hope-He-Don't – Beat-Me too Much-Today

The-Beating – I-Had-Yesterday
Left-Me-Bleeding – Inside
I-Wish-I-Had – Enough-In-Me
To-Escape – My-Endless-Pain

But-I-Am – Only a Dog
That-Needs a Human
To-Take-Care – And-Love-Me

(Chorus)
I Was Suppose To Be
Your Best Friend
But A Human – Monster
Like You Is So Inhuman
Because You Can't Love
Even A Good – Dog Like Me

I-Scratch – The-Couch
Jump-On-The-Bed
Look-Out – Every-Window
That-I – Can-Get-To
It's-My-Thing – The-Way-I-Am

Can't-Wait – 'Til-Night
They-Let-Me – Roam-Totally-Free
The-Sounds – The-Sights
Drives-Me – Feline-Wild
Think-I'll-Go – This-Way-Tonight

(Chorus)
I May Not Have Known You
But I Meant You No Harm
Why Did You Hate Me So Much
And Kill Me In The Night
You're Such A Human – Monster
That You Could Not – Let A Good Cat
Like Me Live – Another Night

I'm-Walking – Down-The-Road
Doing-My-Feline – Night-Time-Thing
And-You – Come-Along – In-Your-Car
Seeing-Me – Makes-You-Laugh
As-You-Drive – Towards-Me
So-You – Can-Smash-Me
Into a Bloody-Mess

I-Hope – My-People – Can-Find-Me
Maybe-They-Can – Help-Me
I'm-Not-Hurting so Much-Now
The-Pain is Lessening – As-I
Begin to Die – Are-You-Happy-Now
You-Human – Monster

(Chorus)
I May Not Have Known You
But I Meant You No Harm
Why Did You Hate Me So Much
And Kill Me In The Night
You're Such A Human – Monster
That You Could Not – Let A Good Cat
Like Me Live – Another Night
71

34. Justice

See-Them – Gather-Around
This-Poor – Dead-Little-Girl
Who a Moment-Ago – Was-Playing
She-Didn't-See – Hear or Pay-Attention
To-The-Car – That-Was-Coming
Straight – Towards-Her

Now-She's-Squished and All-Bloody
What a Horrible-Sight – Too-Real to Be-True
Ran-Over – By a Drunk-Driver
Who-Backed – Back-Over-Her
Then-Drove-Off – Like a Low-Life-Coward

(Chorus)
Justice – Where Is It
Our Little Girl Is Dead
Justice – How Can There Be
When They Still Live
Justice – Where Is It
Our Little Girl Is Dead

People-Out of Their-Homes
The-Girl's – Parents
Mother-In-Shock and Screaming
Father-Running – After-The-Car
Praying to Heaven as Well as To-Hell

He'll-Make a Deal to The-First-One
That-Will-Let – His-Hate – Unite-With-Fury
To-Have-The-Power to Catch-Up to The-Driver
Take-Them-Out – Where-He – Makes-Them-Stop
For-What – They-Have-Done – There-Can-Be
Nothing-Else – This is The-Only-Justice

(Chorus)
Justice – Where Is It
Our Little Girl Is Dead
Justice – How Can There Be
When They Still Live
Justice – Where Is It
Our Little Girl Is Dead

Justice (2.0 Version) (687.)

She-Was so Young – Just-Playing
Loving the Life – She-Lived
Along-Comes – Her-Death
Driving-Drunk – In a Car

Crashing-Sound – Mixed-With a Thump
Makes-Life – Seem-Like a Dream
A-Nightmare – That-Has-Taken-Control
This-Moment of This-Very – Sad-Sad-Day

(Chorus)
Don't Drive Drunk
Let A Little Girl Live
Don't Drive Drunk
Maybe – You Won't Kill Her
Don't Drive Drunk
Maybe – Someone Won't Scream For
Justice – Justice – Justice

Had a Bad-Day – Have a Drink
It's-Your-Life – It's-Your-Right
No-One-Should – Try to Take-It-Away
Then-Again – By-Being so Stupid
You-Make-Their-Case – For-Them

Drinking and Driving – Might-Be-Fun
If-The-World – Was-Made of Non-
Kill-Able-People – Animals and Things

Call a Taxi – You-Drunk – Piece of Crap

(Chorus)
Don't Drive Drunk
Let A Little Girl Live
Don't Drive Drunk
Maybe – You Won't Kill Her
Don't Drive Drunk
Maybe – Someone Won't Scream For
Justice – Justice – Justice

(Repeat Chorus)

73

35. 3 Can Corn Man

Just-Standing in Line
Minding-My-Own-Business
Looking to Score
With-One of These-Sexy
Grocery-Store – Shopping-Ladies
I'm-Hot – I-Always – Stare-Away
From-The-Needy – Ugly-Ladies
No-Matter – How-Much – They-Beg

Bam – Bam – Bam **(Gun Shots)**
Out of Nowhere – I'm-Pissed
Three-Masked – Gun-Wielding
People-Killing-People – Done
Come a Shooting – Themselves on In
Freaking – Damn – Terrorists

(Chorus)
You Might – Have Guns Ready To Shoot
But In The Mist – Of Your Hostages Is A
Pissed- Off-Man – Ready-To – Bring-You-Down
They're Gonna Call Me – The 3 Can Corn Man
After I – 3 Can Corn – You Three Down

Typical – Cowardly – Monsters
Yelling-Away – Raging-All-Up
Putting-Their-Guns – In-People's-Faces
They-Pay-Me – No-Heed – I'm-Far
Enough – In the Back-Ground

I-Wait – Like a Caged – Beast
They-Don't-Know-Me – They-Are-Three
Men-With-Guns – I'm-Just-One – Pissed-Off
Man – With 3 Cans of Corn – In-My-Hands

(Chorus)
You Might – Have Guns Ready To Shoot
But In The Mist – Of Your Hostages Is A
Pissed- Off-Man – Ready-To – Bring-You-Down
They're Gonna Call Me – The 3 Can Corn Man
After I – 3 Can Corn – You Three Down

Thump – Thump – Thump **(3 Cans of Corn Thrown)**

One-Two-Three – Down-They-Go
3 Cans of Corn – Upside-Three – Terrorist's-Heads
Scared-Shoppers in Shock – Afraid to Scream – As-I
Make-My-Way to Gather-Up – Three-Terrorist's-Guns

They-Look at Me – Unbelieving – That-Just a Man
In a Crowd – Beat-Them-Down – Unarmed
Looking at Them – Like-They're-Nothing
Representing-Myself as The-Pissed-Off
Man – That-Doesn't – Take-Any-Shit

(Chorus)
You Might – Have Guns Ready To Shoot
But In The Mist – Of Your Hostages Is A
Pissed- Off-Man – Ready-To – Bring-You-Down
They're Gonna Call Me – The 3 Can Corn Man
After I – 3 Can Corn – You Three Down

I-Don't-Have-Much – Freaking-Broke – All-The-Time
But-I'm an American – Like-Me or Not
I'm-Out-There – Ready to Protect
Myself-That-Is – Get-Over-It
By-Saving-Myself – I-Saved – All of You
Thank-Me – By-Giving-Me – Some-Damn-Money

(Spoken)
The-Hell-With-All of You – Calling-Me
The 3 Can-Corn-Man – It's-Pissing-Me-Off

(Jingle In Shops Near You)

Get-Corned-Up – With-The 3 Can-Corn-Man
Can-Corn-Do-It – Oh-Yes-He-Can
With 3 Cans of Corn – In-Hand – He's-Ready to Strike
Take-Over – For-The-Good of Every-One
Of-Us-Blessed-Americans – God-Bless-America
And-God-Bless – The 3 Can-Corn-Man
Wherever-You're – Corning it Up
Good-Luck and Stay-Corned

75

Yesterday Was Not So Great (806.)

World-Likes to Bleed
All by Mankind's – Design
Blood's – Been-Flowing-Freely
Since-The-Dawn of Time – With-No
Hope of Ending – Any-Time-Soon

Swallowed-Up by Guilt
Life – Love – Hope and Lust
Are-Just – Four-Letter-Words
That the World – Disclaims
In-Every-Way – Every-Single-Day

(Chorus)
Yesterday Was Not So Great
Even Though It Is In My Mind
Living In The Past – Is A Blast
Helps Me Forget What's Coming Tomorrow
That There Are – Less Of Them Everyday

Freedom is a Heavy-Unwanted-Burden
Follow in Line – You'll-Shine so Bright
Just-Like-Everyone-Else – That is Not-Like-You
Smile-Never-Frown – There is No-Other-Way
Difference-Shall-Not – Be-Reborn to You

Time to Celebrate – That
Your-Choices – Are-Fewer
In the Need of Something-New – Just-Ask
We'll-Be-Glad to Tell-You-No – With-Dismay
Smiling as We-Put – Your-Name and Face
On-Our-Thick – List of
Those-That-Won't – Comply

(Chorus)
Yesterday Was Not So Great
Even Though It Is In My Mind
Living In The Past – Is A Blast
Helps Me Forget What's Coming Tomorrow
That There Are – Less Of Them Everyday

36. Empty Hands

Glass-Shattering – Alarms-Blazing – The-Sounds
Of-My-Life – Come-Alive – In-The-Night
My-Heart – In-My-Throat – I'm-In-Ecstasy
Gotta-Get-Going – The-Cage – Would-Kill-Me

Breaking-The-Law – Is-The-Only-Way
I-Know-How-To – Make a Living
I-Like-Trinkets – Gold and Diamonds
These-Are the Tricks of My-Trade
I-Snatch it All-Up – Really-Quick
Then-Run-Away – Even-Quicker

(Chorus)
You Have A Lot Of Stuff
And My Hands Are Empty
As Soon As You Leave
I'll Take What I Need
Sell It On The Streets – For I Need
Some Dough Man – My Hands Are Empty
Please Fill Them – With Lots Of Money

The-Siren so Close – Men in Blue on My-Heels
I'm-Flashing-Fast – Running-For-My-Life
I'm-Too-Slow – Everything is In-My-Way – I-Give-'Em
The-Slip – I'm-Going to Make-It – Out of This-Alive

No-Warning-Shot – Just a Bullet – In-My-Head
I've-Done-My – Last-Dash – I'm-Dying
While-Never – Making-Anyone-Bleed
I-Guess-This-Proves – That-Money is Worth
More-Than-My-Life – To-Hell – With-All of You

(Chorus)
You Have A Lot Of Stuff
And My Hands Are Empty
As Soon As You Leave
I'll Take What I Need
Sell It On The Streets – For I Need
Some Dough Man – My Hands Are Empty
Please Fill Them – With Lots Of Money

37. Evil Pill
(This Song is a What if – Hopefully this Pill will Never be Created)

Scary-Looking-Man – Comes-Up to Me
Says-He's-Got – Whatever-I-Need
Asked if I – Was-Looking – To-Be-Up or Down
So-Many – Different-Colored-Pills
To-Choose-From – I-Can't-Decide

He-Keeps-Rolling-Out – Quantities
And-Prices – He's so Fried
I-Can't-Keep-Up – I-Ask
What-Was-The-Third – One-Again

(Chorus)
Don't Blame Me
It Was The Evil Pill
I Took It And It Made Me
Change – It's Not My Fault
That I Am Now – Addicted
To The Wonderful New Evil Pill

Scary-Man-Starts-Laughing
Tells-Me – He's-Got
Something-Really-Special
Something-Really-New

I'm-The-First-Creature
That-He's – Going to Let-Try
This-Big-New-Sensation
A-Great-Big-Red-Pill
With a Black D
And-Skull Bones – Printed-On-It

(Chorus)
Don't Blame Me
It Was The Evil Pill
I Took It And It Made Me
Change – It's Not My Fault
That I Am Now – Addicted
To The Wonderful New Evil Pill

He-Gave-Me – Four-For-Fifty
Told-Me-Not to Take
Them-All at Once – Yeah-Right
He Doesn't-Know-Me

I-Can-Handle-Anything
Munch-Down a Couple
Nothing – Gobbled-Down
The-Other-Two
Few-Minutes-Later
I'm-Destroying – Everyone-In-Sight

(Chorus)
Don't Blame Me
It Was The Evil Pill
I Took It And It Made Me
Change – It's Not My Fault
That I Am Now – Addicted
To The Wonderful New Evil Pill

Few-Hours-Later
I-Wake-Up – In-Jail
Covered in Blood and Stinking
With-This-Red – Substance
Oozing – Out of My-Mouth

Now-What-The-Hell
Am-I-Gonna-Do
Tell-Them-The-Truth

(Chorus)
Don't Blame Me
It Was The Evil Pill
I Took It And It Made Me
Change – It's Not My Fault
That I Am Now – Addicted
To The Wonderful New Evil Pill

38. Bam Burn Dead Hell
I. The Sighting
II. The Vision
III. Future Burning People Of This Earth

I. The Sighting

It-Was-Standing – In-Front of Me
A-Dark-Figure – With
Red-Burning – Eyes
Hissing at The-Night

The-Smell of Death
Spewing-From-It
Making-Me-Feel-Sick
I-Fall to The-Ground – Having
Prophecies – Inserted-In-My-Mind

I-Raise – From-My-Daze
No-Trace – Death – Is-Gone
Did-This – Really-Happen
Was-This – Just a Dream
Have-I-Become an Outlet-For
Evil – Sick – Hate and Death

The-Thoughts – It-Put – In-My-Mind
Have-Changed – Who-I-Am
So-Many-Deaths – This-World
Has to Avoid – Including – The-Big-One

(Pre-Chorus)
Bam – Bam – Bam
Burn – Burn – Burn
Dead – Dead – Dead
Hell – Hell – Hell
Do You Know What I Am Saying

(Pre-Chorus)
Bam – Bam – Bam
Burn – Burn – Burn
Dead – Dead – Dead
Hell – Hell – Hell
Do You Know What I Am Saying

II. The Vision

Hello-World – Welcome to
The-Vision of Visions
Years – I've-Tried to Focus on
What was Real – and What
Was in My-Mind
Then it Became – Too-Clear-That
I was Dead – Inside
My-Soul was Gone

My-Soul – Now-Lives in Hell
The-Vision – I-Had – Was-I
Returning-From-Hell to Warn-Myself
That the End is Coming to End the World

Nothing – I-Can-Do – Nothing – I-Can-Do
World's-Going to Die – From-Lots of Fire
It-All Starts – With-One-Bomb – Then-Another
Earth-Gets-Pummeled – Earth-Cracks in Half

The-Vision – I-Had – Was-Not for The-World
The-Vision-I-Had – Was-For-Myself
I-Have-Little-Time to Make-Things-Right
So-That-When – I-Die – I-Get to Go To – Heaven
Instead of Burning in Hell – Forever

(Pre-Chorus)
Bam – Bam – Bam
Burn – Burn – Burn
Dead – Dead – Dead
Hell – Hell – Hell
Do You Know What I Am Saying – Now

(Pre-Chorus)
Bam – Bam – Bam
Burn – Burn – Burn
Dead – Dead – Dead
Hell – Hell – Hell
Do You Know What I Am Saying – Now

III. Future Burning People of This Earth

Welcome to My-Mind
You-Won't – Have a Good-Time
In-Here – There-Are-No-Lies
Just-Brutal-Truth – Where-Maybe
Then-Again – And it's Okay – Don't-Exist
For-All-You – Future-Burning-People of This-Earth
Time to Go-Out Have a Good-Time
'Cause-In a Little-While – We-Will-All-Die

Don't-Believe-Me – What-Can-I-Say
I've-Seen-The-Future – It-Involves-Fire
Still-Don't-Believe-Me – Well-Then
Here-You-Go – You-Bunch of Bloody-Fools

(Pre-Chorus)
Bam – Bam – Bam
Burn – Burn – Burn
Dead – Dead – Dead
Hell – Hell – Hell
Do You Know What I Am Saying – Now

Understand and Sing-Along – With-Me
Everybody-Come-On – Scream-It-Out
Stand-Up and Shout-It – Out-Loud
Ready – 1-2-3 – Let's-Burn

(Chorus)
We Are – We Are – The Future
Burning People Of This Earth
No Time To Waste – For We Have To
Get That Last – Great Thing Out Of Us
We Are – We Are – The Future
Burning People Of This Earth
No Time To Cry – About It – For Burning
Death – Is Coming To – Burn Us All Away

(Repeat Chorus)

Alright -Everybody – Thanks-For-Dying – With-Me
It-Has-Been-Great – Not-Knowing-You
Maybe-Our-Essence – Can-Rebuild-This-World
Too-Bad – We-All-Had to Die – Now-For-Our
Final-Goodbye – Here-We-Go

We-Are – We-Are – The-Past
Future-Burning-People of This-Earth
No-More-Us and Them or You and I
We-Are-No-More – That's-It – Goodbye

(Chorus)
We Are – We Are – The Future
Burning People Of This Earth
No Time To Waste – For We Have To
Get That Last – Great Thing Out Of Us
We Are – We Are – The Future
Burning People Of This Earth
No Time To Cry – About It – For Burning
Death – Is Coming To – Burn Us All Away

Come-One – Come-All – Better-Hurry-Up
There-Is a Total – Burning-Earth-Day-Sale
Going on Today – For the Whole – Universe
If-You-Hesitate – All-The-Choice – Cuts of Meats
Will-All be Bought-Up so What-Are-You
Waiting-For – First to Come – First to Be-Served

(An Alien Restaurant – Far Away – From Earth)
Sizzle-Sizzle / Human-Bacon-Anyone
Is-That-Tough / Here-Try-This-One – Is-That-Better – Good
Enjoy-It / Come-Back-Anytime – We-Have-Plenty of
Fresh-Human-Bacon – For-Everyone to Eat / Next-Please

(The jingle that is playing in the background)
Hu-Hu – Human – Ba-Ba – Bacon – Is so Fun to Eat
We-Cook it Up so Great – For-You and Your-Family
Sandwiches-Made – How-You-Like-Them
Mega-Packs – For-Big-Time – Good-Times
The-Humans – Blew-Themselves – All-Up
And-We-Got to Pick-Up – All-The-Savings – For-You
Hu-Hu – Human – Ba-Ba – Bacon – Is so Fun to Eat
Come-On-In and Enjoy – Whatever-Kind of
Human-Bacon – You-Want to Eat – Today

39. Freaking Zombies

Freaking-Zombies-Man
Out-Having a Good-Time
Now-The-Dead – Come-Back to Life
Start-Eating-Everybody's – Flesh and Brains
Now-Instead Of Having – Lots of Sex
Now-Tonight – I-Have to Deal-With
Freaking-Zombies-Man

Blind Date is Hot – She-Wants to Get-It-On
You-Know – I'm-Always-Ready to Please
We-Get in My-Car – She-Shows-Me – Her-Tits
Love-Bone of Mine is Ready to Sexy-Party
I-Slip-My-Hand – Between-Her-Thighs
She-Screams – Like a Scream-Queen
Scaring-The-Hell – Out of Me

(Chorus)
Freaking Zombies Man
Out Having A Good Time
Now The Dead – Come Back To Life
Start Eating Everybody's – Flesh And Brains
Now Instead Of Having – Lots Of Sex
Now Tonight – I Have To Deal With
Freaking Zombies Man

Stupid-Undead-Things – Hunger-Must-Be so Strong
Making-Them-Stand – Right in The-Way – Moaning
When-My-Squishing – Zombie-Car – Rolls-Over-Them
Eat-This – You-Beeping – Undead-Freaking-Zombies
There-Starts to Be – Too-Many to Run-Down
So-Like a Smart-Man – With a Hard-On
I-Turn-The-Corner as Fast as I-Can

(Chorus)
Freaking Zombies Man
Out Having A Good Time
Now The Dead – Come Back To Life
Start Eating Everybody's – Flesh And Brains
Now Instead Of Having – Lots Of Sex
Now Tonight – I Have To Deal With
Freaking Zombies Man

Hitting a Parked-Car
I-Grab – My-Blind-Date
Start-Running – Down-The-Road
She-Too-Damn-Slow – There's-Twenty
Zombies – Up-Ahead and Hungry

I-Say – Hell-With-It
Next-Time – For-Sure
As-I-Throw – My-Blind-Date
To-The-Zombies – Saying-Sorry-Baby
Looks-Like – You're-Din-Din
Wish-I-Could – Have-Had-You-First

(Chorus)
Freaking Zombies Man
Out Having A Good Time
Now The Dead – Come Back To Life
Start Eating Everybody's – Flesh And Brains
Now – Instead Of Having – Lots Of Sex
Now – Tonight – I Have To Deal With
Freaking Zombies Man

I-Learn – Quick
No-Reasoning – With-Zombies
There's-Only – Three-Options

Run-Away – Take-Their
Heads-Off – With-Something
Or – Give-Them – Someone-Else
Tasty to Eat – Down to The-Bone

(Chorus)
Freaking Zombies Man
Out Having A Good Time
Now The Dead – Come Back To Life
Start Eating Everybody's – Flesh And Brains
Now Instead Of Having – Lots Of Sex
Now Tonight – I Have To Deal With
Freaking Zombies Man

40. Set Loose on Hell

I-Was-Supposed to Be – The-Last-One
Special – The-Chosen-One
The-One – That-Won – The-War of Purgatory
I-Was-Screwed – Over-By-God
He-Had – Angel-Eyes-Kill-Me
Which-Sent-Me – Straight to Hell

After-Everything – I've-Been-Through
Now-God's – Not-Done – With-Me-Yet
One-More-Holy-Mission – For-Me to Do
Screw-It – What-Choice – Do-I-Have
I've-Already-Killed – Thousands of Purgatorians
What's-Killing a Bunch of Demons and Satan to Me

(Chorus)
I'm Set Loose On Hell
Have To Take It Over
Start A New Regime
I'm Set Loose On Hell
I Am To Destroy Satan
Become The New Ruler Of Hell

Wonder-Which-One – I'll-Feel-First
The-Burning or The-Freezing – Don't-Matter
I-Can-Take-Anything – Coming-My-Way
It's a Long-Fall to Hell – Satan's-Taking-His-Time
Bet-He-Has – Big-Plans for Me

I-Finally – Reach-Hell – So-Many
Demons in Waiting – They-Attack – With-Fury
I-Keep-Putting – My-Fist-Through-Them
One-After-One – They-Fall-Down-Dead
Looking-Up – There-Are-Thousands of Demons
Roaring-Hell – Trying to Intimidate-Me

(Chorus)
I'm Set Loose On Hell
Have To Take It Over
Start A New Regime
I'm Set Loose On Hell
I Am To Destroy Satan
Become The New Ruler Of Hell
86

No-Satan in Sight – Must be Hiding
This is Going to Take – Too-Long
I-Start-My-Rage-Up – I-Kill-Even-Faster
Sacred-Demons – Step-Back in Fear
Confusion in Their-Eyes – Watching
While-I-Kill – Their-Brothers and Sisters

I-Roar for Their-Submission
Most-Stop – Some-Still-Don't
I-Kill-All-Those – That-Do-Not-Comply
When-I'm-Through – With the Most-Vigorous
I-Command the Rest to Stay-Put – Wait-For-Me
To-Bring-Them – The-Head of Satan
Years is My-Journey – Through-Hell

(Chorus)
I'm Set Loose On Hell
Have To Take It Over
Start A New Regime
I'm Set Loose On Hell
I Am To Destroy Satan
Become The New Ruler Of Hell

Satan's-Waiting – In the Last-Part of Hell
He-Looks as Scared as The-Hell-He-Rules
He's-Talking – Like-I'm – Nothing to Him
Satan-You're-Now – My-Bitch – Kneel – I'll-Make
Your-Death-Quick –Resist – I'll-Rip-You-Apart

Satan-Brings-Forth – Every-Bit of His – Hell's-Fury
Does-No-Good – God-Made-Me – One-Tough-Mother
Tough-Enough to Kill-Satan – With-My-Bare-Hands
I-Beat-My-Chest – Roar-Like a Beast
Showing-Off the Bloody – Dripping-Head of Satan
I-Call-Out to God – Throw-Him-Satan's-Head
Tell-Him to Stick-It – Up-His-Ass
To-Piss-Off – I'm-Through-With-Him
And-His – Holy-Freaking-Missions

(Repeat Chorus)

I-Now-Rule-Hell – Things-Are-Going-To-Be-Different
God-Better be Very-Afraid – Because-He-Is-Next
Wonder-How-Heaven-Will-Look – When-I-Set-It-On-Fire

Rock Don't Hurt (622.)

Night-Time – Coming-Down
Time to Hit – The-Strip
Going to Catch-That
Sweet-Scent of Some-Fine
Sweet-Hot – Ladies-Desire

Going to Keep-Rocking
'Til-I-Taste – Her-Fire
Feeling – Her-Flames of
Hot – Sweet – Desire

(Chorus)
It's Time To Rock And Roll
Because I Know That
Rock Don't Hurt
It Only Makes Rolling
A Whole Lot Better
So Let's Rock And Roll
'Cause-Baby – Rock Don't Hurt

Lipstick – On-My-Thick
My-Pants – Un-Zipped
The-Rocking and Rolling
Is so Fine – This-Night
I-Might-Just – Party-'Til-Dawn

With-Real-Smiles and Fake-Names
Our-Minds – Are-Humming
As-We – Say-Our-Goodbyes – And
Same-Time – Tomorrow-Night

(Chorus)
It's Time To Rock And Roll
Because I Know That
Rock Don't Hurt
It Only Makes Rolling
A Whole Lot Better
So Let's Rock And Roll
'Cause-Baby – Rock Don't Hurt

Rock Fever (Can You Feel It) (750.)

Down-In-The-Dumps
Life's – Dragging-You-Down
You-Just-Don't – Feel-Like
Getting-It-On – Do-You-Baby

Baby-Have-I – News-For-You
Baby – I'm a Large-Size
That-Don't – Give a Love
'Cause – All-I-Want is Some

(Chorus)
Rock Fever – Rock Fever
Can You Feel It – It's In Your Soul
Rock Fever – Rock Fever
Baby – Let's Rock Fever – Together Forever
Rock Fever – Rock Fever
Can You Feel It – It's In Your Soul
Rock Fever – Rock Fever
Baby – Let's Rock Fever – Together Forever

You-Feel – Better-Baby
Rock-Fever – Will-Do-That for You
Come-Here-Baby – I-Got-Bad-News
You're-Cooling – Down-Baby

There's-Good – News-Baby
All-You-Gotta – Do-Baby-is
Take-Me – Two-Times-Baby
'Cause – All-I-Want is Some

(Chorus)
Rock Fever – Rock Fever
Can You Feel It – It's In Your Soul
Rock Fever – Rock Fever
Baby – Let's Rock Fever – Together Forever
Rock Fever – Rock Fever
Can You Feel It – It's In Your Soul
Rock Fever – Rock Fever
Baby – Let's Rock Fever – Together Forever

Sun is Shining-Down on Me
Its-Warmth – Stirs-My-Being
The-Place for My – Fade-Away
Has-Become – Uncomfortable
Making a Tune – Come to My-Mind

Rock – Rock
Rock-And-Roll-House
Rock – Rock
It's-A-Rock-And-Roll-House

I'm-Coming-Back to Life
As-This-Tune – Switches
To-Another – Great-Jam
Laughing-Out-Loud
Enjoying – My-Rebirth

Work-Hard – Party-Harder
Sleep a Little-Bit
Eat-When – I-Have-The-Time
I'm-The-Ready – For-Anything
And-Can-Go – Anytime
Rock-And-Roll – Bachelor
Come-Rock-And-Roll – With-Me

The-Last-Rocker is Back
I'm-Better – Than-Ever
I'm-Feeling – Up-For-Life
When-I-Remember – My-Song
The-Sadness – The-Loneliness
That-Drove-Me to My-Fade-Away

Nobody-Wants to Hear – My-Songs
This-Singing – Guitar-Playing-Nomad
Has-No-One to Play-For
Without-Noticing It I've-Become
The-Last-Rocker

I'm-Almost – Deep-Down
Into a Bad-Case of Mind-Funk
When-Something – Inside-My-Mind
Remembers – Something-Important
About – Someone-Important
When-He-Did – His-Thing
So-Many – Long-Years-Ago

What-Was-It – Who-Was-It
I-Can't – Quite-Remember
It's-On-The-Edge – Of-My-Mind
I-Almost – Got-It
The-Words – Are-Beginning to
Come to Me – I-Remember-Now
Let-Me-Share – Them-With-You
My-Lonely and Sad-World

It's-Not-For-Sale
At-Any-Price
But-It's-Totally-Free
Reach-In-Deep
Pull-Something-Out
That-Is-Exclusive to You
Come-On-Everybody
Let's-Do-Some – **Mind-Rockin'**

I-Feel – Damn-Good
I-Felt – What-I-Sang
So-Much – That-I-Want-To
Sing-Those-Lyrics – One-More-Time

It's-Not-For-Sale
At-Any-Price
But-It's-Totally-Free
Reach-In-Deep
Pull-Something-Out
That-Is-Exclusive to You
Come-On-Everybody
Let's-Do-Some – **Mind-Rockin'**

The-Gemini-One – Did-His-Thing
Now-It's – The-Last-Rocker's
Time to Make a Rockin'-Impact

Nobody-Wants to Hear – My-Songs-Anymore
This-Singing – Guitar-Playing-Nomad
Has-No-One to Play-For
Without-Noticing-It – I-Have-Become
The-Last-Rocker

This-Sadness – Infected-My-Mind
Made-Me-Question – My-Purpose
'Til-I-Said – Forget-It-One-Day
And-Tried to Fade – My-Life-Away
Due-To so Many – Long-Years
Of-Rock and Rolling by Myself

I-Stopped – Fighting-The-Heavy
Letting it Take-Hold of The-World
While-I-Was – Trying to Share
My-Rock and Roll-Songs
With-Anybody – That-Would-Have-Me

(Chorus)
I'm The Last Rocker
I Was Born On One Rockin' Day
I Felt Pleasure – I Felt Pain
I Lived Hard – I Got Laid Lots
Living My Rock And Roll Dream
Now I'm Going To Stand Up Tall
Once Again And Rock And Roll
This World 'Til It Remembers My Name

Rock and Roll – Has-Turned-Into-Silence
The-Inner-Mind of The-Individual
Is-What-Matters – The-Most
To the Massive-Mass of People
That-Live – Life-All-Alone

Watching-The-Few – That-Still
Enjoy-Life – With-Closed-Minds
Having-No-Interest – In-Joining-Them
The-Party – Never-Gets-Started
Rock and Roll – Has-Turned-Into-Silence

My-Rebirth – Has-Brought-Back
My-Youth – I-Feel so Alive and Fine
When-I – Look-Into-The-Mirror
I-See-Freedom – Wrapped-Anew – Around
An-Old-Way of Life – That's-Been-Forgotten
But-Very-Soon – Will be Remembered by The-World

(Chorus)
I'm The Last Rocker
I Was Born On One Rockin' Day
I Felt Pleasure – I Felt Pain
I Lived Hard – I Got Laid Lots
Living My Rock And Roll Dream
Now I'm Going To Stand Up Tall
Once Again And Rock And Roll
This World 'Til It Remembers My Name

I-Turn-My-Songs – Into-Poems
Reading-Them – Out-In-The-Streets
Day 1 – I-Made an Impact
Day 2 – I-Had a Good-Crowd
Day 10 – I-Got-Paid – For-My-Words
Day 13 – I-Picked-Up – My-Guitar
Playing-Along to My-Words

Now on Day 18 – I-Walk on Stage
With-The-Power of Mind-Rockin'
Something-New – That-Turns-Into
Something-Old – Rock and Roll
By-The-End of The-Night
Rock and Roll – Is-Alive – Breeding-Freedom
Into-My-Fans – Minds and Hearts
Proving – Rock-And-Roll – Will-Never-Die

(Chorus)
I'm The Last Rocker
I Was Born On One Rockin' Day
I Felt Pleasure – I Felt Pain
I Lived Hard – I Got Laid Lots
Living My Rock And Roll Dream
Now I'm Going To Stand Up Tall
Once Again And Rock And Roll
This World 'Til It Remembers My Name

We Are Here (Original Version)

You-Have – Made-Us-Bleed – For so Long
That-We-Have – Almost-Wilted-Away
There-Are-No-More – Tears to Cry
You-Have-Almost – Destroyed-Everything
It is Time – For-You to Stop
Your-Way-Leads to Nothing – But-The-Same
We-Have-Lived and Died – Enough-For-You

We – Are – Here
We-Want to Be-Truly-Free
But-We-Are – Tied to This-World
Stop-Making so Much – Killing-Things
And-Start to Make – Living-Things
No-More-Poison – Waters and Lands
It-Is-Time to Take – The-Ugly-Out
And-Bring – The-Beauty-Back-In

We – Are – Here
We – Are – Here
We – Are – Here
How-Many-Times – Do-We-Have to Say-This
Do-We-Have to Start – Our-Own-Church
No-More-Damn-Blood – For-You-Monsters
If-You – Won't-Change
Then-You –Will-Have to Go-Away
Power-We-Will-All – Take-Away-From-You
We – Are – Here – And
We-Are-Here to Stay

You-Better – Fear-Us
What-Will-Start – As a Group
Will-Walk – This-Earth
One by One – Will be The-Way
It-May-Take – Many-Years
But-Our-Time – Will-Come

No-One-Man – Country or Power
Can't-Stop-This – It-Is-About – The-We
The-True – We-The-People
Not of One-Country
But of This – Whole-Earth

We-Have-Had-Enough
No-More – Letting-People-Kill
Or-Hoard-Things – That-Do-That-For-Them
The-Time – Has-Long-Passed
For-The-Sayings
"That-Is-How-It-Is" OR
"It-Ain't-Never – Going to Change"

What-The-Hell – Kinda of Concept is That
We-Have-Brains and Hearts – Don't-We
No-More – No-More
Killing – Just-For-Killing
Just-For-Someone's – Heaven's-Sake

We – Are – Here – And-It-Is
Time to Let – The-Rest of You-Know
How-It-Is – Going to Be
If-You-Finally – Want to Start-Livin'
And-Make-The-World – Better-For-Your-Families

No-More-Destruction
No-More-Murder
No-More-Rape
No-More-Hunger
No-More-Taking of Innocence

Just-More of Tolerance
More of Happiness
More of Love
More of Understanding and Rights
Rights-That-Only – Apply to The-Good
Evil-Starts to Die – This-Day
It-Is a Heavy-Burden
That-We – Bring-Down-Upon-Us

We – Are – Here – And-We
Took-The-First-Step
It is Up to You – The-Future
To-Keep-This – Going-On
Don't-Let-This-End
'Til-It-Is-The-Way – It-Is-Meant-To-Be

The Invention Of Mind Rockin'

I've always been a fan of music, classic rock, rock and roll, hard rock and heavy metal. I've also always been a fan of movies, comedy drama, action, suspense, fantasy and horror. As a kid my hobby was writing lyrics that I created in my mind. In 2013 I took my hobby, my passion for music and movies and with them I created Mind Rockin'. By doing so I made myself become something that I never thought or dreamed of doing before and that was to become a self-published author. My creation of Mind Rockin' works like this. I sit down in front of my computer and come up with a melody or score in my mind to go along with the original songs or lyrical stories that I am creating. However when you the reader/singer reads or sings the song or lyrical story, there is no right or wrong for the melody or score that you come up with in your minds, be it rock and roll, pop, country or rap. Mind Rockin' is a concept I created for persons just like myself, those of us that would like to be able to do or create something like stories or songs but with no opportunity knocking at the door this dream of ours stays that, a dream. Mind Rockin' is the only thing in the world where the person you are has the chance to use what's inside you instead of the usual way where it is only one way for everybody, and that is the way the creator intended for it to be foretold or heard.

I'd like to dedicate this book and thank my Wife of Twenty-Four years, I love you Christina thank you for your Love and Support.

I'd like to thank all my Family and all my Friends. Thank you to all my Fans, I am a Fan of yours as well, together We can make a difference. Let's Shout It Out and Speak As One.

The Gemini Rising Rockin' Machine.

Your Very Own Mind Rockin' Love or Sexy Song

Your Very Own Mind Rockin' Political or Social Song

Your Very Own Mind Rockin' Fantasy Song

Your Very Own Mind Rockin' Horror Song

www.ingramcontent.com/pod-product-compliance
Lightning Source LLC
Chambersburg PA
CBHW070510130626
46555CB00003B/1238

9 780615 900315